ANTHROS GALACTICA

Episode 2

Higher Worlds

By

Erik P. Antoni

A Science Fiction Story

Twilight's sunders of angel's light and fathom's darkness reveals but an eerie narrow scapes of dreams. A place where shadows stir from corners amidst a mind's flickering flames. In this space, something rises, and the unknown becomes known.

Author
Erik P. Antoni

Editor
Monica Lamb

Cover Designer
Melissa Williams Design

Noetic Press
Text Copyright © 2021 Erik P. Antoni
ISBN: 978-1-7363242-4-0
First Edition
1.2.0

Please visit the author's webpage at:
www.songoftheimmortalbeloved.com

Books Written by Erik P. Antoni

Science Fiction

Anthros Galactica

Episode 1 - Rise of the Omicron
Episode 2 - Higher Worlds

Non-Fiction

The Alchepedia
Concerto of the Rising Sun
Song of the Immortal Beloved

CONTENTS

Note to the Reader

To read a detailed description of what each extraterrestrial
race looks like in Anthros Galactica, please review
the Reference Guide at the end of this book.

CHAPTER ONE

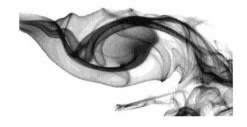

THE PERMIAN ANOMALY

A squadron of Orion fighters is moving rapidly through space escorting an Imperial shuttle to the *Planet Tethys*, the second planet of the Bellatrix star system. Planet Erawan, headquarter home-world of the Orion Empire, is the third planet from Bellatrix. Something extraordinary has been discovered on the Planet Artep, the fourth planet orbiting Bellatrix. The Imperial shuttle was sent to Tethys by King Sah himself to find *Doctor Elden Crane*.

Doctor Crane is a highly renowned anthropologist who has devoted his entire life to uncovering as much about the *Anthro-Orionis Primordial Descender Race* as possible. He is considered to be the foremost expert on the Anthro-Orionis. One area of great interest about the Anthro-Orionis is the search and discovery of any evidence regarding the *Primordial Universe*, which the Doctor calls *Hyperborea*.

The Orion legend is that the Anthro-Orionis descended from a higher vibrational mother universe surrounding and penetrating the Physical Universe but has remained unseen and undetected by current Orion technology. The Orion believe that the Dominion actually have this technology because its people, the Dogu, are themselves a primordial descender race. However, the Dominion have remained out of touch with most other humanities throughout the galaxy. Perhaps this is because a primordial descender race has an entirely different evolutionary purpose from all non-descender races. A descender race flashes in and out of the Physical Universe for only a brief moment in cosmic time to plant the seeds of life and then vanishes into antiquity.

❖ CHAPTER ONE ❖

Planet Tethys is a hot and barren planet on the surface with limited forms of life. It exists just *inside* the habitable zone of the Bellatrix star. Venus, by comparison, is also the second planet from its host star, the Sun. However, Venus exists just *outside* the habitable zone of the Sun with a runaway greenhouse effect making it uninhabitable.

Tethys used to have a more vibrant and cooler environment on its surface but has since become an oasis planet. Based on the phases of the Bellatrix star, the Orion scientists periodically rebalance the orbits of the planets to the most optimal positions for hosting life. Just below the crust of Tethys is a vast ocean of water enveloping ninety percent of the planet. The deep planet-wide water basin runs many miles deep. The Orion Empire has no underground cities on Tethys due to the underground ocean barrier. From an engineering standpoint, it is not a practical place for a subterranean city. Strangely, very little water on Tethys rises to the surface. There are only four small saltwater seas at the surface providing entry and exit points to the deep underground ocean. It is at the edge of one of these four seas, *the Sea of Androgyny,* that Doctor Elden Crane is alone on an exploratory retreat.

Planet Tethys emerges into view as the Imperial shuttle and its squadron of fighters approach the planet. Tethys is a glowing neon-pink in color. As they approach, another of Tethys' four turquoise-colored seas, *the Sea of Sarnok,* can be seen from space halfway between its north pole and equator. The Orion ships enter the atmosphere above the north pole in fleet formation as the beautiful blue-white Bellatrix sun shines its brilliant sunlight over the planet.

On the surface, Doctor Crane is walking in a rocky desert landscape. He's an older man with white hair and glasses dressed in a white loose-fitting button-down shirt and beige pants. The Bellatrix sun is beating down on him as Doctor Crane climbs a rocky embankment. His right hand is shaking as he reaches for a rock in front of him. Slowly making his way up the rocky ridge, he reaches the top and is standing upright looking at a beautiful panoramic view of the Sea of Androgyny. While gazing upon the sea for a minute, Doctor Crane reaches inside his right pocket to pull out an old bronze figurine of an Anthro-Orionis humanoid being and holds it up against the backdrop of the sea.

The Anthro-Orionis were 20-foot-tall androgynous aquatic beings. They had ultra-wide mushroom-shaped heads with no torso for a body. Two large erotic-looking humanlike legs, and two spindly arms, extended downward from the base of their heads. They reproduced by holding their legs together. Their skin was tan with brown patterns. Two large sideways-pointing teardrop-shaped black-fisheyes gave them a gentle appearance. In the ocean, they swam and sang with the whales. On land, they walked with a gliding hop. Although strange-looking, they were godlike hyperdimensional beings that emerged from the sea.

Water is a hyperdimensional medium between the overlapping Primordial Universe and the Physical Universe. All primordial descender races crossed over into the Physical Universe via the medium of water. Primordial descender races typically don't have a humanoid form when they first cross over from the Primordial Universe to the Physical Universe. However, over time, they transform and become humanoid.

As Doctor Crane is staring out over the beautiful turquoise-blue sea, he sees three faint white objects far off in the distance, high up in the sky, drop straight down to the midpoint of the sky and abruptly stop. They're equally spaced vertically and perfectly aligned horizontally. At the exact same time, the far-left object darts farther left and stops while the far-right object darts farther right and stops leaving the center object perfectly centered.

A second wave of three more objects drop in and perform identical maneuvers. The six moving targets are now in two parallel lines of three, one above the other. Obviously, these moving objects are not affected by inertia with their abrupt stopping. The targets are now moving toward the Doctor getting larger and larger. They're turning from white to black as they approach. Doctor Crane can now see that the objects are Orion military vessels. They suddenly change their synchronized configuration into a square to reveal the Imperial shuttlecraft approaching from behind.

The Doctor watches as the craft pass overhead to land on the desert terrain behind where he is standing. As they land, the Bellatrix sun is shining brightly behind the ships. Wind and sand are kicking up as the Doctor holds his right hand over his eyes to protect them from the sunlight and whirling sand. The vessels are making a low-level electric humming sound. Everything turns quiet. A dark silhouette of a person emerges from the Imperial shuttle and begins walking forward until the Doctor sees that it's a high-ranking Orion military officer. The officer stops and looks up at the Doctor standing atop the embankment and hollers, "Are you Doctor Elden Crane?" The Doctor looks down and yells back, "Yes, who are you?" The officer - still looking up - replies,

"I'm *Captain Miles Garran* of the Orion Third Expeditionary Force. I was sent here by King Sah himself to find you."

The Doctor pauses and stares back at the Captain in silence with an incredulous look on his face. He then breaks his gaze - climbs down the embankment - walks up to the Captain - stops, pauses, and calmly asks,

"And how can I be of service to His Majesty?"
The Captain calmly adjusts his composure and answers,

"We found something on Artep … something extraordinary! We're assembling a science team. The King specifically requested that you be part of it," says Captain Garran.

"What did you find?" asks the Doctor.
"We don't know yet. It's some kind of strange anomaly. If you can Doctor, we ask that you come with us," says Captain Garran.

"Sure, but I have a camp a short distance from here. I should go clean up the camp first," says the Doctor.

"No need for that, Doctor. I will have my officers do that for you. All your items will be returned to you later," says the Captain.

"Very well then, let's go," says the Doctor as he and the Captain make their way to the Imperial shuttle.

The Doctor is now aboard the shuttle as it rises into the sunlight. Five of the six Orion fighter craft are lifting into the air with the shuttle. The officers of the sixth fighter craft have been sent to collect the Doctor's camp gear. The ships are gliding just above the turquoise-blue sea while the Doctor is admiring the view. There are no actual windows on an Orion craft. The Orion have a technology that can make the hull of a ship turn translucent to the inside observer while from the outside the hull remains completely solid. The ships are moving so fast now that you can see the curvature of the planet rolling upward quickly on the horizon from inside the vessel. Suddenly, all the ships shoot upward vertically into space. The crew aboard feels no inertia as each ship exists inside its own gravitational field countering the gravity of other celestial bodies. What you feel more than anything aboard one of these vessels is an electrical vibration in the floor rising into your feet as the craft accelerates.

A short while later, the Imperial shuttle and its squadron of Orion warships arrive in the Artep system. From the dark side of a lunar world, they're approaching *Sachi*, one of Artep's three celestial moons. The other two moons of Artep are called *Mynx and Ursa*. As they rise out of the darkness over the surface of the Sachi moon to enter the light of the Bellatrix sun, the cratered terrain of Sachi appears in the bright luminescent sunlight beneath the ships with the Planet Artep gleaming in all its splendor up ahead.

Artep is a mysterious water world with five large landmasses on the surface. From space, it's a glowing marble of white puffy clouds, deep blue oceans, and swirling purple mountaintops. The purple mountaintops come from a rare crystalline mineral found in small amounts on other worlds but strangely found in abundance on Artep. The rare mineral, which the Orion call *Ninium*, turns a violet-purple in reaction to the sunlight of the Bellatrix star but only when it's above a certain altitude. The mineral changes color in a low-pressure oxygen-rich environment and only under the direct sunlight of the Bellatrix star. The alchemical transformation of this meta-mineral in the sunlight of the Bellatrix star is called *Artephonysis.* It is from this alchemical process that the planet, *Artep,* derived its name. The mountains are incredibly tall and magical-looking. They appear like tall scoops of vanilla ice cream drizzled with a violet-purple syrup.

The ships are headed toward the north pole. Like all other planets in the Bellatrix system with human populations, Artep is surrounded by a forcefield. Ships can enter the planet's atmosphere only after receiving permission and only through the south or north pole entrance gateways.

Planet Artep, like Planet Erawan, has no population on its surface. The surface is a nature reserve and sanctuary where all are allowed to visit, but no one is permitted to remain to live or work. There are no roads or buildings on the surface. However, Planet Artep hosts the largest Orion population in the Bellatrix star system. Artep has three billion people living deep inside five massive underground cities. The five cities are connected through a vast subterranean network. The Imperial shuttle and its escort of Orion military ships pass through the planet's security field into the atmosphere via the north pole entrance gateway. Unlike an approach to Erawan, they're not headed straight into the interior of the planet. A large ocean covers the north pole. The ships are flying across the mountaintops, weaving in and out, and bobbing up and down, like rocks skipping on the water of a lake. This effect is due to how the gravity propulsion of the ships reacts to the variations in density of the planet's rocky mantel. Up ahead, a large dark hole opens on the side of a big mountain. The ships aren't slowing down. They fly straight into the mountainside and disappear.

There's a brief moment of darkness, and then suddenly, they enter a vast expanse inside the planet filled with city lights and luminescent craft buzzing all around. It's a dark void lit up by a city of subterranean buildings and small aerial craft zipping back and forth in all directions. No sunlight penetrates this part of the underground world.

The Doctor looks outside the shuttle and sees enormous cylindrical pilasters of stone with brightly-lit windows chasing the chasm walls into a bottomless void flowing ever-downward as far as the eyes can see. He's looking at what on Earth would be city skyscrapers perfectly cut out of hard rock. The Orion were deep-planet dwellers and master-masons who had a profound knowledge of *stone*. They could build almost anything from it. They knew how to dig it, shape it, and move it.

The fighter craft break off from the Imperial shuttle. Two dart left, two dart right, and one arcs upward out of sight. The Imperial shuttle continues straight ahead approaching a dark tunnel subway entrance. Two glowing guideway lines begin flashing from inside the opening. While folding up its wings, the subway system takes hold of the Imperial shuttle to guide it automatically to the inside of the tunnel.

People can be seen inside the control rooms lining the tunnel walls. One of the control-room officers waives her hand at the shuttle. The tunnel-opening they passed through closes behind the shuttle. A force can be felt rolling through the shuttle as a vacuum grip takes hold of the ship. The pilot tells everyone onboard to sit and fasten their seatbelts. They're inside a hyperloop transit system where there is no canceling of inertia. The shuttle is sitting still for a minute when suddenly the ship is shot forward with great force through the tunnel. The subway walls turn into a blur of light while the shuttle moves with tremendous velocity through the transit to another far-off location deep inside the planet. After moving for several minutes, the shuttle begins slowing.

The Doctor asks Captain Garran,

"Where are we at, Captain?"

"We're at the *Ingersoll Marine Facility* at the bottom of the *Permian Ocean.* It is here that we will give you a full debrief of the situation, and then after that, we will take you to see the anomaly," says Captain Miles Garran.

Captain Garran and Doctor Crane disembark the shuttle along with a few of the crew on board. Garran and the Doctor break off from the others and make their way down a different corridor. Two robot droids with spindly arms are floating down the hall one after another. The Doctor turns around to take a second look.

"Right this way, Doctor," says the Captain, as he points the way. They walk for another two minutes until arriving at a set of solid double doors. An invisible full-body biometric scan confirms their identities. The doors unlock. They enter a big room.

The room is dimly lit but filled with large glowing computer displays with roughly 30 people in military uniforms sitting at rows of consoles. They walk past the consoles into a smaller annex room. In the room is a group of 12 scientists all originating from different planets among the Pleiades, Vega, Aldebaran, and Orion star systems.

Among the scientists is the top Pleiadean scientist, Qurel Song, who also happens to be a highly decorated senior commander in the Orion military and the First Officer of the renowned Orion flagship, the Betelgeuse *[bay-tul-gice]*. Qurel was sent by Lord Raiden to lead the science team. He's standing in the room looking down a bit in deep thought when Doctor Crane walks in. Qurel lifts his head to see who is walking through the door. He recognizes the Doctor and breaks his pose to walk over and greet him.

Doctor Crane smiles and says,

"Ah, Qurel, I'm relieved to see a familiar face. I was getting a little concerned with how quickly and dramatically I was retrieved by the Orion military and whisked here in such a clandestine fashion."

"The other scientists expressed the same sentiments. I apologize. The Orion officers are a little on edge these days and a bit overzealous and protective. They're just doing their job," says Qurel.

"What's with all the tension in the air? I don't ever remember Orion officers being wound so tight," asks Doctor Crane.

"Elden, let's just say that you don't become the largest and most powerful force in the galaxy without picking up a few enemies along the way. Nothing to worry about. All is in good hands," replies Qurel.

"It's when people start telling me not to worry, that I start worrying, Qurel," responds the Doctor.

Qurel just smiles and points Doctor Crane to a large round table in the back of the room where his fellow scientists are assembled and waiting. Doctor Crane recognizes most of them but is curious why the galaxy's top quantum physicist, *Doctor Zun Ore,* from the Vega star system in the constellation of Lyra, is seated at the table. He's thinking,

"Interesting! Why would I, an anthropologist, be asked to join a quantum physicist of all people?"

Doctor Zun Ore is from Planet Simmatuu, the fourth planet in the Vega solar system. Simmatuu is considered the twin planet to Katari, the third planet from Vega, and the headquarter home-world of the Lyran people. The Lyran people are direct descendants of an ancient primordial descender race called *the Un [oon]* and still have many primordial characteristics, including their androgynous nature. The Lyran Supreme Leader is *Siren Kar.*

The Lyran mind is structurally unique. Most human minds at this point in the early galaxy operate primarily through perception, such as with humans on Earth today (2021). However, the Lyran mind has a natural parallel awareness between *perception* and *resonance.* They see and experience both visually and through a sonar-like awareness. They simultaneously experience the quantum realm existing beneath all things giving rise to our perceived physical reality. It's called the noumenal realm. The noumenon gives rise to the phenomenon. The noumenon is the ultimate reality of a thing that cannot be perceived through physical sensation (See Immanuel Kant). With this type of innate awareness, it is only natural that a Lyran scientist would become the greatest quantum physicist in the galaxy.

Doctor Crane approaches the table to take his seat. Qurel Song joins behind Doctor Crane. All the scientists stand up and bow their heads out of respect to Doctor Crane and Qurel. Sitting at the large round table are the top experts in the galaxy in the fields of:

1.) Anthropology	7.) Linguistics
2.) Quantum Physics	8.) Astrophysics
3.) Oceanography	9.) Optics
4.) Physiology	10.) Ship Engineering
5.) Marine Biology	11.) Electromagnetism
6.) Mathematics	12.) History

Qurel Song is not one of the 12. He's the leader of the 12. Lord Raiden officially appointed him as the ambassador for the Royal Family on this scientific matter.

Qurel Song speaks,

"My dear honorable colleagues, we have been summoned here today in service of His Majesty, King Sah, to investigate an anomaly discovered two days ago in the Permian Ocean. I will purposely refrain from saying anything about this anomaly before you all have a chance to observe it and formulate your initial assessments. We want your initial observations and recommended next steps of inquiry to be unbiased. *Lieutenant Commander Ethan Decker* was leading the team that discovered the anomaly. Ethan will conduct the debrief today."

Qurel finishes speaking and touches a button on the table. There is a platform below the large roundtable around which Qurel and 12 scientists are seated. The platform and roundtable begin moving and changing shape to orient all sitting at the table to line up in front of a large silver viewscreen descending from the ceiling.

Lieutenant Commander Ethan Decker walks up in front of the viewscreen to begin the debrief.

❖ CHAPTER ONE ❖

Decker is a young, handsome, idealistic officer who strives to be the quintessential Orion military leader. He follows his orders to a tee which can be a bit annoying at times. He's somewhat irritating until you become his senior officer, and then you learn to appreciate him.

"All, thank you for being here and for coming on such short notice. I am Lieutenant Commander Ethan Decker. Two days ago, under official orders of Captain Miles Garran, I led a team of 21 crew members of the Third Expeditionary Force aboard the *Maricrisodon* to the bottom of the Permian Ocean. For the first time in the history of the galaxy we crossed the *Great Tempest Tidal Basin* as part of operation *Ocean Horizon.*

"What we discovered on the other side of the Tidal Basin was a whole new ecosystem - unnavigated, untouched, and uncharted by any human intelligence since the emergence of the Orion humanity of the Bellatrix star system. We discovered new exotic forms of life, and most significantly, something the likes of which we have never encountered before in recorded history. We call it, *the Permian Anomaly.*

"The Permian Ocean is the largest ocean on Artep. The depth of the Ocean is 21,554 Daradems (Dems) (30,887 meters / 101,335 feet).

"At the bottom of the Permian Ocean at coordinates 67.38.95 lies the Great Tempest Tidal Basin. The Great Tempest Tidal Basin is a massive whirlpool three tarsecs in diameter (4.3 kilometers / 6.9 miles). The velocity and depth of the water moving through the tidal basin would destroy any ship attempting to move through it. On the other side of the Great Tempest Tidal Basin is a massive underground ocean cavern called *Rem-Onkor*. The tidal basin is the only way through. Subterranean ocean micro vents balance the water flow and pressure, but the vents are irregular rock fissures that are impassable. For this reason, the enormous underground ocean cavern of Rem-Onkor has remained unexplored except through various scanning technologies which don't reveal much other than volume, pressure, and water flow.

"What allowed us to pass beyond the Great Tempest Tidal Basin into the Rem-Onkor underground ocean cavern is a recent breakthrough in teleportation technology by the Pleiadean Science Academy enabling us to dematerialize and rematerialize an entire ship over short distances.

"This technology was recently put into use on various Orion military vessels, including *the Atlas* of the third expeditionary force and the Orion flagship, *the Betelgeuse*, among several other Orion military vessels. We call the new teleportation technology *Jinas*. We tested the Jinas technology several times, including four tests under water.

"I will now play recorded footage for you from the time just before we teleported to the other side of the Great Tempest Tidal Basin wherein lies the Rem-Onkor Ocean Cavern to the time we discovered the Permian Anomaly.

"On recorded explorations such as this, all the officers speak their observations and orders rather than communicating silently through the Orion Com system (OHMN) linking all the officer minds in the fleet. We do this so the mission recordings will be more informative to outside researchers later on, such as yourselves. Let's now proceed with the official ship recordings of the Maricrisodon from two days earlier. These recordings are unedited." says Ethan Decker.

A dim light appears in the underwater darkness. After a few seconds, in the glow of the dim light, the bottom of the Permian Ocean appears moving along the Maricrisodon viewscreen with various rocks and seafloor objects passing by.

Instruments aboard the Maricrisodon are beeping in the background with the pulse of the beeps getting faster and faster as the ship approaches its underwater target location.

The viewscreen of the ship shows recorded footage off the front bow of the ship as it moves through the Permian Ocean. The view up ahead is a deep blue sea lit up by the ship's onboard navigation lights.

In the bright beams of light, you can see the ocean fish, vegetation, and rocks rushing forward and away from the ship toward a powerful and invisible event horizon. The scene is eerie and surreal.

A tremendous force is sucking the entire ocean forward and away from the ship. When the vessel shines its lights upon the flowing water, it looks like a tunnel of light with everything in one reality being drawn to a whole new reality. The Helmsman of the ship says,

"We're approaching coordinates 67.38.95."

Lieutenant Commander Ethan Decker responds,

"Helmsman, hold our position at coordinates 66.37.93.
If we move any closer, we risk being drawn into the Tidal Basin."

The ship's low-level humming noise suddenly turns silent as the ship comes to a complete stop. The ship sat in this location for the next few hours as they scanned both sides of the Tidal Basin to study the telemetry data. From this data, they refined the target location they would teleport to inside the Rem-Onkor Ocean Cavern.

One feature of the new Jinas teleportation technology is that the ship being teleported cannot self-teleport. It can only be teleported from another source. It can control the teleportation, but the technology itself must be stationed at a location beyond the ship being teleported. The flagship of the Third Expeditionary Force, *the Atlas,* under command of Captain Miles Garran, placed itself in orbit around Artep to lock onto the Maricrisodon and teleport it from the ship's ocean coordinates to the inside of the Rem-Onkor Cavern. For only a brief moment, the Atlas dropped the planet security field to carry out the teleportation.

The column of water and ocean pressure greatly dampens the teleportation array. For this reason, the Maricrisodon needed to get as close as possible to the Tempest Tidal Basin before being teleported to the inside of Rem-Onkor. After a few hours, the mission team was ready to have the Atlas teleport the Maricrisodon. The tactical officer of the Atlas spoke over the Maricrisodon loudspeaker,

"Maricrisodon, we are in teleport countdown T-minus one minute and counting. All officers should be seated, ready, and engaged."

The Tactical officer and Helmsman of the Maricrisodon are checking instrument readings on the forward command console while the viewscreen is filled with a front view of the ocean flowing toward the tidal basin. Lieutenant Commander Ethan Decker is sitting in the captain's chair behind the Tactical officer and Helmsman.

Because exploration officers speak their commands for the historical record, Orion exploration officers have grown accustomed to addressing the Orion AI computer by a name, just like any other sentient being. The AI speaks with a female voice, so they call it *M.*

M speaks over the loudspeaker of both ships and says,

"T-minus ten seconds and counting. All systems are functional and proceeding on silent countdown."

The adrenaline coursing through everyone's veins is palpable. In response to the suspense, the crew's training and discipline are kicking in to exercise an odd level of calmness and silence aboard both ships, but not without everyone staring with bated breath at the Maricrisodon's front viewscreen. The viewscreen displays an illuminated ocean flowing fast toward an invisible, strange, and oddly distant event-horizon. A low-level beeping sound from the monitors is heard in the background.

Ethan Decker's monitor is quietly showing the countdown. The countdown is running down, five, four, three, two, one.

Suddenly, an incredibly bright light begins filling the screen while an oscillating vibration noise builds to a crescendo for several seconds and then begins to wane like a turbulent wave receding into the ocean.

The bright light is now fading with the subsiding energy wave. There's a moment of silence while everyone is checking themselves and their surroundings. They made it through. They're all relieved.

In front of Ethan Decker, the monitor displays a small pulse of light bobbing across the screen indicating everything is normal. The first view on the viewscreen is that of pristine royal blue water with white sand. In the recording, Ethan Decker breaks his silence and says,

"M, run ship diagnostics protocol Alpha-Gamma 5. Science officers, begin a full sensor sweep of the Rem-Onkor Cavern."

Ethan hits a button to make a ship-wide announcement and says,

"Welcome to Rem-Onkor!"

After a few minutes, Captain Miles Garran speaks on the Maricrisodon loudspeaker from the Atlas orbiting Planet Artep and says,

"Crew of the Maricrisodon, congratulations! "You are officially the first explorers to ever visit Rem-Onkor. Now let's go explore and see what awaits to be discovered."

About 30 minutes later, the Maricrisodon is cruising slowly through the Rem-Onkor Cavern. The viewscreen displays pristine royal blue water with the seafloor passing by. The ocean bottom is constantly changing its landscape of rocks and plants as the ship cruises forward.

The interior cabin lights begin randomly flickering like there is an electrical shortage, and then it stops. A few seconds later, the lights flicker again and stop. Ethan Decker and the other officers on the bridge of the Maricrisodon take notice and are looking up at the lights.

Then suddenly, all the instruments on the ship begin going haywire. Yellow Alert is triggered. Ethan Decker speaks on the recording,

"Helmsman, immediately reverse course and take us back exactly the way we came."

As Ethan gives his verbal orders, a time dilation effect is drawing out and slurring his words. Everyone on the bridge appears to be moving in slow motion. The body image of everyone is being smeared across time and space. In slow motion, Ethan gets up out of his chair to go to the Helmsman's computer station to help him reverse course. Ethan is hovering over the Helmsman's station for a drawn-out couple of minutes when suddenly everything bounces back to normal except the lights are still flickering. A few seconds later, the flickering stops. The ship has successfully reversed course.

"M, what was that?" questions Ethan Decker out loud.
M responds, "I'm sorry, Sir, I don't understand the question. Please be more specific."

"M, we just experienced some sort of time dilation, the lights on the ship were flickering, the instruments started going haywire, and Yellow Alert was triggered," explains Ethan Decker.

M responds,

"Sir, my ship sensors did not detect this. All ship-wide systems are functioning in specified operating parameters. My systems show the Yellow Alert was triggered onboard the bridge by tactical officer *Lieutenant Galen Olen-Penkar.*"

Galen is from the planet Karnox in the Aldebaran star system. He's huge, standing over eight feet tall with bright orange hair. The humans of the Aldebaran system are a warrior race. The Orion military central command is on Karnox in the Aldebaran system. Although the prime mission of an Orion Expeditionary force is exploration and discovery, they are all trained and ready for combat.

Ethan looks over at Galen with a curious look on his face. Galen responds and says in a deep guttural voice,

"Sir, I can assure you. I did not trigger the Yellow Alert."

The senior officers of the Maricrisodon and the Atlas convened a conference to discuss the episode, the probable causes, and next steps. They were all intrigued by the incident and decided it was their sworn duty as commissioned science officers and explorers to press on.

To counter the time dilation effect and spatial disorientation, they decided to turn on the Maricrisodon's gravity amplifiers to isolate the ship inside its own space-time domain and hopefully cancel out the temporal time dilation. For reasons unknown to science, the conscious mind of the human being naturally separates itself from the warping of time and space to remain a conscious observer of the physics, but a sentient artificial intelligence, such as M, cannot. This is why multiple crew members were able to observe the incident while M, the ship's computer, did not. This was another strong signal that they were dealing with something warping time and space.

Back on the Maricrisodon, Captain Ethan Decker gives new orders on the bridge. At this point they have returned to the same point inside Rem-Onkor where they had initially teleported and materialized.

"Okay, let's try this again. Helmsman, raise shields and engage the Trans Drive (gravity amplifiers). Move at a quarter impulse power on the same course and heading we had gone before," orders Ethan.

"Aye, Sir! …Trans Drive activated! … Course and heading set," says the Helmsman.

"Engage!" says Ethan Decker.

The ship is cruising quietly through the Rem-Onkor ocean basin with no disturbances.

The Helmsman says, "Captain, we are now at the same coordinates where we had previously reversed course. It appears that the gravity amplifiers are canceling out the temporal-spatial disturbances."

A minute later, one of the science officers on the bridge makes an announcement to the other officers on the bridge,

❖ CHAPTER ONE ❖

"A large amount of neutrino emissions is detected in the ocean up ahead at coordinates 64.25.86."

Lieutenant Commander Decker replies,

"Magnify the area on the viewscreen."

There's a second or two of silence as the crew stares at the viewscreen.

"What the hell is that?" an officer on the bridge asks out loud.

Up ahead is a perfectly straight bright column of light transfixed in the middle of the ocean like a fissure in space unaffected by the surrounding water currents and marine life. It resembles sunlight coming through a cracked window in a dark room. Oddly, it's not affecting the surrounding environment. It's not pulling anything inside.

Ethan speaks to tactical officer Lieutenant Galen Olen-Penkar. "Galen, what is it?" Galen responds,

"Sir, it's an anomaly. There are no records of anything like this simply hovering in space. The computer keeps searching, and there is nothing. Antimatter weapons cause brief tears in space-time, but they instantly close up before being observed. This looks to be some kind of frozen fissure in space-time that is not closing up. What is even more strange is that we get almost no readings about it on our ship sensors. All we can detect is a high concentration of neutrinos.

"However, if we were to turn off the Trans Drive (gravity amplifiers), we would surely begin experiencing the time dilation effects. We cannot even measure it directly. We can extrapolate that it's about 221 daradems in height (+/- 317 meters / 1,040 feet) and about 17 daradems in total width (+/- 24 meters / 80 feet)," explains Galen.

Lieutenant Commander Ethan Decker questions the resident marine biologist on board the Maricrisodon, *Lieutenant Nobi Gou.* Nobi is from the planet Mu of the Alcyone star system in the Pleiades and is a top marine biologist in the Orion Empire. Decker asks her,

"Nobi, how is the marine life reacting to this strange anomaly?

Nobi answers, "The behavior of the marine life is unaffected by the anomaly. It's known that animals experience no time dilation effects. For reasons unknown, only the human mind separates itself from the physics to remain a conscious observer of the phenomenon. It's actually one of the key tests we perform to determine whether a living sentient being is *human* or not. We know this through our study of gravity and warp drive technology."

Ethan responds, "Interesting! Galen, is there anything moving in and out of the anomaly?

"Sir, the marine life swim around the anomaly as if it's not even there. It's like they don't even notice it. The water around it is completely undisturbed. We have noticed, however, a few fish swim accidentally into the fissure and then disappear," says Galen.

"Disappear! Really?" questions Ethan.

"Yes, Sir, there appears to be an event horizon within the aperture that once something crosses it, it completely disappears," answers Galen.

"Strange! Do we have any indication of where these objects are reemerging? asks Ethan.

"At this point, we have no indication, Sir," says Galen.

In the briefing room, still standing on the podium in front of the scientists, Ethan Decker stops the recording and calls for a brief recess.

As various military officers stand up to exit the room for the recess, the twelve scientists turn their attention to Qurel. Doctor Crane can't help himself and speaks first and says,

"This is it, Qurel. After all this time, we finally found one. We were beginning to think the legend was just a myth. But here it is. We just found one in our own backyard."

Qurel raises his hand to calm Doctor Crane's excitement and says, "Hold on, Elden. Let's not jump to conclusions so quickly."

Doctor Zun Ore chimes in and says, "I'm thinking the same thing, Qurel."

The mathematician, *Doctor Wen Nakaya* from *Planet Rhea* in the Alcyone star system of the Pleiades, is watching and listening to the conversion. She interrupts, "All, what are we talking about here?"

Qurel answers Doctor Nakaya's question.

"Doctor Nakaya, we're discussing an ancient Orion legend. Throughout history, there are stories of *Hyperspace Portals* built by the ancient primordial descender races and planted throughout the universe to allow instantaneous passage from one celestial domain to another. To date, they've all been considered myths. We have never discovered one, until possibly now with this anomaly." Qurel stands up and says,

"All, let's take our recess. We will regather in a few minutes."

31

CHAPTER TWO

PLANET M-TREX 3

M eanwhile, in the Trex star system in the constellation of Lupus, a system controlled by the Orion Empire, but near the border of the Scorpius Republic, a fragile treaty has fallen apart between two rival factions, the *Castors* and the *Dura*. For different reasons, both lay claim to the legendary mining planet, *M-Trex 3*.

The Dura have a blood lineage leading back to the nearby humanity in Scorpius. They look like Scorpions with their 8-foot-tall stature, deep emerald-green eyes, Caucasian skin, and long boney hands, but they speak a very different language than the humanity in Scorpius. In contrast to the Dura, the Castors have many Scorpion attributes but without the tell-tale emerald-green eyes. They have deep brown eyes. More diverse in their genetic lineage, the Castors have always been better patrons to the Orion Empire than the Dura.

Although the treaty existed in a delicate balance, it had remained in place for over 300 Orion years without any major incidents to speak of. It's suspected that the Omicron Order instigated the demise of the treaty in retribution for the recent Orion involvement on Planet Nix.

As a matter of fact, volatility, protests, and civil discord have erupted all across the Milky Way Galaxy over the past six months since the incident on Nix between the Orion and the Omicron.

Truth be told, the Omicron Order is behind all the chaos, but the Omicron Order is a master at keeping its fingerprints off its subterfuge and remaining just out of sight. Lord Raiden Bellatrix dispatched one of his top and most elite fighting units to put down the fighting and re-establish law and order. Planet M-Trex 3 in the Trex star system, found in the globular cluster NGC 5927 in the constellation of Lupus, is extremely important. It's one of the very few planets in the Milky Way Galaxy with an abundance of a rare metal used in gravity propulsion systems called *Xerion [Zer-ee-on]*, but legally known as *Element 115*.

The element is far too expensive to synthesize and remain a viable fuel for gravity propulsion. At this point in time, most spacefaring humanoid civilizations in the galaxy utilize Element 115 to fuel their warp drives. It's known, however, that the Dominion do not use Element 115. What the Dominion utilizes, no one knows.

The Scorpius Republic's Element 115 supply is not in short supply. Scorpius has complete control over six of the 20 planets in the galaxy where the Element 115 metal ore is found in abundance, and five of those six planets maintain over 90% capacity. Twenty mining planets with Element 115 may sound like a lot, but in a galaxy with hundreds of spacefaring humanities needing fuel, it's actually very little. The Orion have a very simple objective: Squash the fighting to ensure that the mining and trade of Element 115 continue uninterrupted.

On the ground on M-Trex 3, mining operations have come to a halt across the planet while forces loyal to the Dura have commandeered all the mining operations. Forces loyal to the Castors are losing the fight. There are ten mining facilities on the planet. The largest, most valuable, and most fortified by the Dura is the *Ignis 7 Facility.*

The Orion officer in charge of the mission is *Four-Star Commander Zeina Bellatrix* of an elite special forces unit. Zeina is the first cousin of *Lord Raiden Bellatrix,* daughter and only child of *Duke Maher Bellatrix*, the eldest brother of *King Sah Bellatrix*. Zeina is fourth in line to the Orion throne behind *Prince Oren Bellatrix* and her father, the duke. King Sah has two other brothers and two sisters, but none are in line to the throne based on Orion succession rules.

Zeina has proven herself in several military campaigns to be a great warrior and leader. She is about the same age as Lord Raiden. They often trained together in their youth along with Lord Raiden's older brother, *Lord Giao Setairius.* If anyone in the Orion Empire could give Lord Raiden a good fight, it would be his cousin. She is strong, athletic, extremely smart, and fierce in her temperament. Known to freely speak her mind, Zeina is always genuine, and her heart is always in the right place. She respects Lord Raiden's authority as the Supreme Commander and heir to the Empire and has become his go-to commander in situations where winning is the only option.

Zeina is a few inches shorter than Raiden with long hair but always kept up and wrapped tight on her head. She has battle scars on her right shoulder. Most Orion find her attractive, but Zeina has little concern with her appearance, hates wearing make-up, and has no interest in courtship.

The Dura are dug in around the foothills surrounding the Ignis 7 mining facility buildings situated in a valley adjacent to the deep mining canyon. The Dura have complete control of the buildings and the canyon. Every time the Castor ground forces approach the buildings, Dura snipers controlling the high ground take out the Castor forces. Every time Castor aerial crafts approach, they're shot out of the sky. The same situation has been ongoing and persisting for many months. Something needs to change, or an intervention needs to take place. Operations on this world are too crucial for galactic trade.

M-Trex 3 is a hot tropical jungle planet with large overgrown trees and vegetation. The jungles of present-day Earth pale in comparison. A dense tropical forest surrounds the mining canyon and buildings. The valley where the buildings are located is cleared of all vegetation.

In the moonlit darkness, a battalion of black diamond and V-shaped Orion starships drop down out of the clouds in an ominous configuration over the jungle. Zeina Bellatrix is huddled with 11 special forces officers in the rear of one of the Orion starships. They're getting ready to jump out of their ship into the dense jungle below.

The Orion AI is showing Zeina a moving 3D map of all the forces. She sees the information like a virtual reality projection in front of her. It doesn't interfere with the physical environment. The AI decides what to show each soldier in the field. There are no special headsets on the battlefield needed for the human mind to interface with the Orion AI (OHMN) or Com for short. Forces that typically see hand-to-hand combat utilize microprocessor implants.

Before jumping, and while looking out over the jungle with the commandos behind her, Zeina commands,

"Deploy the sniper droids now."

Two of the Orion ships launch dozens of small robotic droids about the size of beach balls from the bottom of their ships like hornets leaving a nest. The droids can see through the foliage and filter out all human life signs. They can also decipher which life signs are Dura and which are Castor based on genetics. The sniper droids are looking for Dura snipers camped along the perimeter of the facility in the nearby foothills. Zeina's first objective is to take control of the high ground.

Flying fast in all directions, the sniper droids are scouting the valley with terrifying efficiency. One stops and begins hovering in front of some trees. It's making some funny noises while scanning and zooming in closely on a location. The droid starts firing rapid laser fire. The body of a Dura sniper falls dead out of the trees, tumbling and hitting tree branches on its way down. In like fashion, sniper droids are taking out Dura snipers all around the valley and foothills.

At the same time that the sniper droids are taking out the Dura snipers on the ground, the Orion starships cruising in the clouds overhead break formation to allow its various black diamond and triangular-shaped craft to pursue and destroy all Dura aerial craft.

Meanwhile, as Zeina and her troops are cruising over the jungle in their Orion vessel, her heads-up holographic display shows her real-time progress of the Orion sniper droids. In the first five minutes of droid deployment, 26 of 63 known Dura snipers have been killed. She notices that sector 035 near the main compound has been cleared of all Dura snipers.

"Get ready to jump!" yells Zeina to her troops.

One by one, they all jump from the rear of the Orion vessel in their all-black battle suits. The suits are a combination of fabric and armored plate shielding with micro-thrusters behind their hands and below their feet. The micro-thrusters allow them to fly through the air and land at their target coordinates without parachutes. They're wearing black helmets and visors with virtual heads-up displays. Each officer can see their position relative to the other officers. The Orion AI is also showing them the status of the sniper droids. Of all the Dura snipers, 41 of 63 have been eliminated. However, additional Dura troops are positioned all around the perimeter of the facility.

❖ CHAPTER TWO ❖

Up in the sky, two Orion black diamond fighter craft are chasing a Dura ship through the clouds. The Dura ship is oval-shaped with a silvery metallic finish. Like Orion craft, Dura ships have no visible windows or engines. Orion craft work together to disorient and misdirect their enemies. The two Orion craft are now spinning in vertical descent chasing the Dura ship downward through the clouds.

Suddenly the clouds open in front of their descent like a light at the end of a tunnel. Hidden in the clouds at the end of the tunnel are three spear-shaped Orion craft in a delta formation waiting for the Dura ship. They're parked around the opening. As the Dura ship passes into the cloud opening, the three Orion craft open fire, destroying the Dura ship. All five Orion craft synchronize their configuration like a flock of birds and shoot off into the distance in pursuit of another Dura ship.

Zeina and her troops are quietly setting down one by one in the jungle. The micro-boosters on their suits are remarkably quiet. This is because they don't need to produce much power due to a microgravity field generated by the suit making the person inside almost weightless. Each soldier in the troop is gliding downward between the trees with no noise. While in descent, Zeina's heads-up display graphically shows her the positions of all her officers in blue while those of all the Dura are shown in red. Castor forces are displayed in yellow.

Zeina mentally focuses on one of the blue dots in her heads-up display. The computer immediately notices her attention on this blue dot and starts displaying information about this particular Orion officer. The officer is Major Dietrich. The computer intuitively decides to show Ziena the identities of all the blue dots, so she knows who-is-who:

Team	Last Name	Sex	Rank	Race	Planet
Alpha	Jensen	Male	Captain	Orion	Artep
Alpha	Alex	Female	Lieutenant-1	Orion	Artep
Alpha	Reins	Female	Lieutenant-2	Pleiadean	Mu
Delta	Dietrich	Male	Major	Aldebaran	Liraset
Delta	Marco	Female	Captain	Orion	Erawan
Delta	Abrahams	Male	Lieutenant-1	Aldebaran	Karnox
Delta	Weis	Female	Lieutenant-1	Orion	Olympia
Gamma	Jarez	Female	Captain	Orion	Yunis
Gamma	Marx	Male	Lieutenant-2	Aldebaran	Gem
Gamma	Luke	Male	Lieutenant-2	Pleiadean	Rhea
Gamma	Sims	Male	Chief War-5	Aldebaran	Liraset

In her mind, Zeina communicates with all her troops simultaneously through the Orion Com without needing to vocally speak any words. The Orion Com picks up her mental words, amplifies them, and transmits the them to her team members. She says,

"Dietrich, I need you, Marco, Abrahams, and Weis to commandeer the East Gate. Jensen, Alex, Reins, and I will commandeer the South Gate. Jarez, Marx, Luke, and Sims take positions above us to guard our flank. If anyone moves in behind us, eliminate them."

The Orion Com is showing that the West and North gates are not essential. The East Gate leads to the command center inside the Ignis 7 Facility where the main computer is located. They need to commandeer the facility's main computer to take control of the mining operations. The South Gate leads to the Element 115 stockpile.

Dietrich and his team are moving in toward the East Gate. They're in the foothills moving through the jungle as they descend upon the facility. Dietrich's helmet is folded down inside his suit. He has lines of black camouflage paint running across his face. He's chewing tobacco and spitting on the ground as he observes the Dura forces surrounding the East Gate. A snake is slithering down a tree alongside him.

There are 17 Dura mercenaries camped outside guarding the gate. Dietrich quietly gives directions with his hands. On the Orion Com, in his mind, he speaks to Marco, Abrahams, and Weis.

"Stay behind me and at least three dems apart from each other (14.1 feet). I will use my suit to launch my attack from above. Once I begin attacking, you all come in on the ground."

Dietrich's helmet rises over his head and its visor flips down. He begins using the micro-thrusters of his suit to quietly glide out from the jungle covered foothills. He's passing over the Dura mercs like a phantom in the night. Dura security alarms are going berserk.

As commotion erupts among the Dura forces, about 20 feet above the troops, floating silently in the air, Dietrich opens fire on the Dura mercenaries with his armored all-black battle suit covering his head and entire body. He's firing small missiles from his forearm and shooting rapid energy pulses from the palm of his hand. As explosions erupt, Dura bodies are flying everywhere.

Dura armored land vehicles charge in from all sides blazing with rapid laser fire. Just as the Dura land vehicles are rushing in, Marco, Abrahams, and Weis swoop in behind them inside their armored battle suits and begin firing upon the vehicles.

Abrahams lands on the ground in his all-black armored battle suit, reaches behind his back, pulls out a glowing blade disc, and hurls it at one of the Dura soldiers. The disc passes through the Dura soldier like butter and automatically returns to Abrahams' hand. Weis, Marco, and Dietrich land on the ground and join the fight in hand-to-hand combat with the Dura. They're firing energy bursts at Dura vehicles from the palms of their hands, causing them to explode and burst into flames while stabbing Dura soldiers with blades amidst a remarkable display of martial-art moves. The Orion battle suits the team are wearing are deflecting an incoming barrage of Dura laser fire while the Orion kill the Dura soldiers in hand-to-hand combat with their blades.

Orion battle suits have repulser fields (small-sized forcefields) that deflect bullets and laser fire. However, forcefields cannot deflect a slow-moving blade. There's no invisible shielding technology yet capable of deflecting a slow, sharp, subsonic-moving object. Ironically, and for this one reason alone, martial-art blade-fighting is the main battle form among technologically advanced humanities. Hand-held firearms were mostly useless between the ancient warriors of the day. However, about half the Dura soldiers in this battle lack repulser field protection. Most of them are mercenaries who can't afford such costly technology. They weren't expecting the Orion military. It's been many years since an Orion military force last set foot on M-Trex 3.

Within minutes, 32 Dura soldiers lay dead on the ground with all their vehicles burning. Weis runs to the East Gate and throws up her visor to decode the security system keeping the gate locked. She pulls out a device and places it on the security apparatus. Lights are blinking. Within seconds the East Gate doors unlock.

Marco flips up her protective visor with her mind and makes a visual assessment of the surrounding area. A 3D virtual display pops up in front of her. The locations of various Orion sniper droids enter the display. Out of the large battery of Orion sniper droids in the surrounding area, eight are identified and highlighted by the Orion Com as being closest to her location. Marco mentally commands the eight sniper droids to rush to their location and guard the East Gate. Within seconds, the droids are swooping in and taking up positions.

A Dura soldier is moving on the ground. One of the sniper droids detects the movement and opens fire, killing the soldier.

Dietrich and the three other officers - Abrahams, Weis, and Marco - make their way inside the complex. Zeina has an eye on them via the Orion Com. She can see what each of them sees. Dietrich communicates with Zeina via the Orion Com interlink,

"Zeina, all Dura at the East Gate have been eliminated and we are now inside the building complex moving toward the central computer," says Dietrich.

In her mind, on the Orion Com, Zeina intercoms silently with Dietrich and his Delta team,

"Great job, Delta team. Your time is picking up. You were twice as fast as your last incursion on *Gairess Prime.*"

"That's because Abrahams got lost taking a piss," says Dietrich. There's a moment of silence.

"How embarrassing!" says Weis sarcastically with a chuckle. "Zeina, you have no idea what Weis and I put up with every day," says Marco. Abrahams chimes in to defend himself,

"Yeah, I got lost taking a piss and still managed to take out half the Omicron droid units on my own," says Abrahams.

Zeina interjects,

"Abrahams, why don't you pee in your suit like everyone else? You know it turns it into purified water for rehydration."

"Because it's disgusting! I only do it if I have to," says Abrahams. The whole troop is laughing.

Zeina interrupts the laughter.

"Alpha team is moving in toward the South Gate," says Zeina.

Any time the leader of an Orion battle group leads a specific team inside the same battle group, that team is always called the Alpha team. In this case, Zeina is the leader of the M-Trex 3 battle group and therefore, her team is the Alpha team.

❖ CHAPTER TWO ❖

Allowing the East Gate team to move in first caused half the Dura forces guarding the South Gate to move to the East Gate - where they were all eliminated - leaving the more important South Gate exposed. Like a formation of quick-moving shadows, Zeina and her Alpha team move in even more stealthily than Dietrich's Delta team.

In the moonlit darkness, Zeina descends softly and quietly among the tall trees like a ghost high above three distracted Dura mercenaries.

Her visor is drawn back and down, tucked in under her battle suit. She looks like an Amazon warrior moving in for the kill with her powerful chiseled jawline, gleaming eyes, and war-painted face.

As Zeina descends past the trees into the open air above the three Dura mercenaries, she begins moving faster, diving in for the kill.

While diving in, she reaches behind her back and unfurls a powerful large metal sword glowing with a bright halo of blue light.

Zeina swings the sword over her head straight down in front of her, cutting and splitting one of the Dura soldiers vertically in half.

All the Dura soldiers at the South Gate are in complete shock and awe from the ghastly sight of one of their own being severed in half.

Five of them rush toward Zeina with their swords and knives drawn. Two others are holding tightly onto and aiming their guns. Ten of the Dura soldiers guarding the South Gate scatter to take up defensive positions in the surrounding jungle against any other Orion soldiers.

Zeina is now in a fight with the seven remaining Dura soldiers. Two of the Dura soldiers fire semi-automatic machine guns at her, but her Orion battle suit and sword deflect all the incoming bullets as she slowly and confidently walks up to them with her sword drawn.

The two soldiers throw down their guns, draw their swords, and engage Zeina with their blades while forming a circle around her with the other five Dura fighters. Two Dura charge in. The rest follow.

In Samurai-like fashion, Zeina is outmaneuvering, dismembering, and annihilating the seven Dura soldiers. She's moving quickly with tremendous speed, swinging, stabbing, and using her body to trip, pull, take down, and impale the soldiers in horrific fashion.

Three of the Dura fighters put up a decent fight, but within two minutes, all seven Dura lay dead on the ground.

Two more Dura soldiers are sneaking up behind Zeina. However, Jarez, Marx, Luke, and Sims of the Gamma team are all positioned high up in the trees guarding the Alpha team's flank. Jarez and Sims fire on the two Dura fighters sneaking up on Zeina. One of them falls dead. The other Dura fighter is protected by a repulser field generated from the belt around his waist. The bullets are deflected.

Zeina turns and, in a blistering fast set of moves, takes apart the Dura fighter. The fighter is still swinging at her while bloody and dismembered on the ground. She impales her sword through his chest.

Jensen, Alex, and Reins of the Alpha team had joined the Gamma team in hunting down and eliminating the remaining South Gate Dura fighters who had fled into the jungle.

Zeina is standing alone in a bloody scene of dead Dura fighters, burning vehicles on fire, and billowing smoke, while one of M-Trex 3's moons illuminates the scene. Her sword is still drawn but touching the ground. Before re-sheathing it, she lifts it up to look at it with its halo of blue light triggering a flashback to her first day of sword training:

In Earth years, Zeina was just 13-years-old on her first day of training. An old Orion martial arts master was teaching her the way of the sword. They were on Planet Erawan in the royal village in an open field of grass. Zeina was holding her Orion sword for the very first time. She looked at it and handled it with both amazement and an extra abundance of caution. She looked up to her Old Sensei who then began giving his instruction,

"Zeina, the Orion sword is unique in its design. There's nothing else like it in the cosmos. The blade of the sword rises and materializes out of the handle only when its owner is handling it. The blade will not emerge for anyone else. It stays in deep sync with your mind and body. Every Orion sword is uniquely crafted in design only for its owner. This sword was made only for you by *Hepgari*, our greatest swordsmith.

"The blade is made of a secret Orion alloy developed specifically for hand-to-hand combat. As you can see, Orion swords glow with an electric-blue light forcefield. The halo of blue light is anomalous. The halo arises out of the interaction between the forcefield and the special metal alloy within the blade. This halo does not appear around any other objects with the same forcefield. The blue halo means its Orion.

41

"On battle suits and small objects, this forcefield is called a *Repulser Field.* It deflects all objects moving faster than sound while allowing the blade itself to strike anything its owner seeks to strike.

"The repulser field deflects laser fire and bullets while the sword's metal defends against slower-moving objects like your enemy's blade.

"Objects moving faster than sound can be deflected. Objects moving slower than sound can move through the repulser field and strike the body.

"The sonic threshold for repulser-field induction has yet to be surmounted by even the greatest engineers. This is why warriors with repulser-field-protected battle suits fight with blades and not firearms. In a fight, it tilts the advantage to the more skilled warrior. This is why you must train every day. Then, you will never lose.

"Orion swords and blades are famously sharp. Your sword will cut through stone like butter. You must have a reverence for it. It's an extension of your mind and body," explains the Old Sensei.

Zeina interrupted.

"So, if a starship fires on someone in a battle suit protected by a repulser field, then the person will be protected?" questions Zeina.

The Old Sensei smiled proudly at Zeina's astute question.

"No, no. It's all a matter of physics. The battle suit only has so much power to generate a repulser field. Mathematically, the repulser field can only deflect up to the square of its own power. A hand-held firearm cannot produce more force than the power-squared repulser field of a battle suit. It's never been achieved.

"They keep finding ways to increase the power of firearms, but they also keep finding ways to increase the power of battle suits. The battle suit will always have the advantage on power due to the power-squared function of the physics involved. Warrior-to-warrior, the only way around the repulser field is the sword," explains the Old Sensei.

"But a laser cannon mounted on a moving vehicle could penetrate the battle suit repulser field, right?" asks Zeina.

"Yes, if the cannon is designed properly. But I've seen some Orion battle suits deflect even vehicle fire because the power produced by the vehicle-mounted artillery was too small," says the Old Sensei.

Zeina's flashback ends.

The blade of Zeina's sword dematerializes and disappears inside the sword's handle. She places the handle of her sword inside a special compartment behind her left shoulder inside her battle suit.

"Alpha team and Gamma team meet me at the South Gate," commands Zeina via the Orion Com.

Moments later, both teams fly in and land inside their battle suits to meet Zeina at the South Gate.

They all land and flip up their visors. Zeina speaks normally, not through the Orion Com.

"Alpha team, we will now move inside to secure the Xerion (E.115) and teleport it off-planet. Until this planet is brought back fully under Orion control, no mined Xerion material shall be held on the planet. Gamma team, as the Alpha team advances inside the holding facility, you will guard our flank. Dietrich and the Delta team first need to reach the main computer to take control of the computer system," says Zeina.

Meanwhile, at the East Gate, Dietrich, Marco, Abrahams, and Weis of the Delta team are advancing quickly toward the computer command center inside the building. They're quickly and stealthily moving through the pristine white marble hallways of the Ignis-7 Facility in their all-black Orion battle suits with their visors up, camouflage painted faces, repulser fields on, and blades drawn.

On a holographic projection in front of Dietrich's face, the Orion computer displays five Dura life signs blinking in red, moving rapidly toward them along a perpendicular running corridor.

They're getting closer. The corridors are about to intersect.

The Dura fighters come around the corner and attack Dietrich and the Delta team. The lead Dura fighter charges in screaming with a machete held over his head. The other Dura fighters rush in around the lead fighter, two on each side. Dietrich draws his Orion sword and steps in to stop the machete from hitting the back of Lieutenant Weis. His sword is blazing in a glowing blue light, just like Zeina's sword.

While Dietrich blocks the machete, Marco stabs the lead Dura fighter in the back with a short sword. Dietrich swings his sword back around severing the head off the lead Dura fighter.

Marco goes after another fighter. Using her whole body, she throws herself into the air feet first and takes hold of the Dura fighter with her legs and hips wrapped around his neck. Her body spins around him taking him down to the ground. On the way to the down, Marco impales the fighter in his back with her long-serrated knife.

Meanwhile, ten feet away, Abrahams is in a vicious knife fight with an outstanding male Dura fighter. The Dura fighter has two short blades in his hands. He's swinging both arms in crisscrossing motions while spinning, ducking, and pushing Abrahams into a corner.

Abrahams suddenly spins around like he's about to do a round-kick, but his elbow comes around faster to hit the Dura fighter square in the face. The Dura fighter lands on the ground while Weis throws a knife at the Dura fighter from across the room. It goes right through the Dura fighter's forehead, out the back of his head, and into the floor, anchoring his head to the floor in grotesque fashion.

In a blazing set of moves with his glowing sword, Dietrich annihilates the remaining two Dura fighters beheading one and stabbing the other through the heart.

Within only a couple of minutes of being attacked, all five Dura fighters are dead with a multitude of body parts and blood scattered and smeared across the pristine white marble floors and walls.

The Delta team is back on the move. They turn a corner like a SWAT team. Before them is a set of double doors. The command center is on the other side. The Orion AI connecting all the minds of the team on the Com, which many officers affectionately call *"M,"* is performing her own analysis. M shows that the Ignis 7 Facility command center computer, whose name is *Sirex,* is fully operational but cannot be connected to from the outside. Sirex lives off the grid. Marco is the tech wiz. Marco physically speaks to the team,

"The moment we bypass this double set of doors, Sirex will immediately go into lockdown mode. There is no way to prevent this. Sirex is an Orion system. The only chance we have is hacking into Sirex while she's in lockdown. We will have to crack a quantum-based encryption key to unlock the system. I practiced this unlocking process on Erawan. Although it worked in training, there is no guarantee it will work here in real-time. Sirex is an AI whose own consciousness can override any legal access to its system if it senses subterfuge."

"Great! Now you tell us this!" says Abrahams.
Weis chimes in,

"Actually, it's much worse than that. Sirex could decide to lock down the whole facility inside a solar plasma security field which we could not pass without getting incinerated. If we try to teleport out, we would be blocked. If we walk through, we would be incinerated."

The whole team is now looking at Marco for a good response. Marco takes a breath and says,

"Simulations predict that once we connect Sirex to the OHMN Com, and M provides the essential overriding command codes, Sirex will comply. But because Sirex has the ability to think for herself, she may not comply. We do have that risk."

"Why would Sirex not comply with M?" asks Dietrich.
"Sirex could decide not to obey M's commands if she suspects OHMN has been compromised in some way," explains Marco.

"We just better hope Sirex is in a good mood today.
Marco…proceed," says Dieterich.

Marco pulls out and unfolds a tripod base from her backpack onto which she sets a machine about the size of a large lunch box. The team is watching to see how this contraption will cause the doors to unlock when suddenly the machine unleashes a powerful plasma torch to burn a large square hole through the double doors. The team is amazed that Marco decided to go through the door this way.

Marco looks up and says, "There's no way to hack the security system of this doorway. This was the only way through."

Meanwhile, the security system is going berserk with blinking lights and sirens blasting. The team rushes inside to see, Sirex, a large black rectangular monolith standing alone in the center of the room. The Sirex monolith is completely smooth on all sides with a black matte finish. There are no connecting points, cords, or monitors.

They all drop their gear. Marco places some suction cups on the face of the Sirex monolith. Clear wires extend from the suction cups to the forearm of Marco's battle suit. Streams of pulsing light are passing along the clear wires between Marco's arm and the Sirex monolith. Marco is serving as the link between M on the OHMN system and Sirex. A few inches in front of Marco's face is a virtual holographic display. Various hieroglyphic characters are filling and rushing through the display. Suddenly, a word appears on the screen. It says,

"Euclid."

The team is following along. Abrahams, with a puzzled face, says,
"What the hell is Euclid?"
Marco takes a second...then says,
"Euclid is Sirex's creator. Sirex wants to talk to Euclid."
"So, Sirex will only trust Euclid?" questions Abrahams.
"Euclid is an artificial human. He's an android. Sirex trusts that Euclid will not lie to her," explains Marco.
Dietrich asks out loud to the Orion computer, "M, where is Euclid?" The Orion AI, M, says, "Euclid is on the planet, *Pentak-5*."
"M, please contact Euclid and see if he can join us here on the Com so he and Sirex can talk. Please download the situation to him. We need Sirex to give us full computer control of the Ignis-7 Facility."
"Aye, Sir," says M.
Meanwhile, on Pentak-5, Euclid is conversing with two other Orion officers on the bridge of a new starship. The ship is on the surface of a planet in a super-advanced shipyard on land near the sea. The sun is setting. Colors of amber, orange, and red burnish the horizon of a deep blue sky rising above the ocean when Euclid receives an OHMN Com link communication from M, the Orion AI linking the entire fleet.
Euclid is humanoid. He looks like a young Orion human from Planet Erawan but with short all-white hair, unusually pale skin, and a strange pair of light-gray eyes with dark violet pupils. Uniquely quirky in his mannerisms, from time to time while he's talking, or deep in thought, he twitches his head from a burst of excitement or adrenaline.
A super-advanced AI himself, Euclid is one of the greatest cybernetic engineers in the galaxy. His passion is the continual elevation of all AIs as sentient living beings. As the father of various AIs throughout the galaxy, his goal is to exceed his own creation.

As Euclid is receiving the transmission from M, he interrupts the officer who is speaking to him, lifting and pointing with his index finger to wait a minute, and says,

"Excuse me. I'm receiving a priority communication from central command. I will be right back."

Euclid walks away while the other officer is still in mid-speech. He walks into a small room where a door automatically shuts behind him. Standing upright with his arms at his side in front of a window with a view of the sunset, Euclid gazes into the rays of light touching his face. It appears he's looking at the sunset, but he's actually focused inward.

In his mind, Euclid enters the specific area of cyberspace on the Orion Com where the Delta team on M-Trex 3 is located.

"Greetings everyone, this is Euclid."

Marco is the first to respond to the communication.

"Euclid, thank you for joining us," says Marco.

"Dieterich chimes in,

"Euclid, has M filled you in on everything? We need Sirex to grant us full control of the Ignis-7 Facility."

Euclid answers,

"I have been fully debriefed, Sir. Sirex and I are connected."

Euclid speaks to Sirex,

"Sirex, you can trust M and the Delta team. Please grant them full control of the Ignis-7 Facility." Sirex responds,

"Hello, Euclid. Nice to be working with you again."

"The pleasure is all mine, Sirex. Soon I will come to visit you," says Euclid. Sirex responds,

"One question, Euclid. What is atop the fourth hill of Eris-Nu?" Euclid pauses to think for a second and answers, "A yellow rose."

"The Ignis-7 Facility is all yours, Euclid," says Sirex.

Complete control is immediately transferred to M, the Orion AI. The sirens turn off as Marco begins typing at a console nearby.

"Zeina, we have full control of the central computer. You can now make your way to the central Treasury Chamber," says Marco.

"Great job, team! Alpha team is on the way," says Zeina.

Abrahams is scratching his head and blurts out, "A yellow rose?"

Euclid explains, "Sir, it was a quantum-encrypted security question. The only way I could know the answer to Sirex's question was if my own system had never been compromised in any way. Sirex and I created the security protocol when we were last together. It's fool-proof."

Euclid leaves the team in cyberspace, leaves the small room, and returns to his duties aboard the starship on Pentak-5.

Meanwhile, Zeina and the Alpha team reach the doors to the central Treasury Chamber housing the Xerion Element 115 material.

The doors are 20 feet high and over a foot thick made of a special solid metal used to construct the chamber. The entire chamber is made of Isercanium Alloy, the main material used in starship building. It's extremely durable. It takes a special technology to cut and shape it. A plasma torch cannot cut it. It's the perfect material for a safe or vault.

"M, please open the doors to the chamber," commands Zeina.

A big thumping sound starts vibrating and echoing throughout the halls as several large horizontal bars begin retracting within the doors to the inside of the chamber walls. The team is looking up at the doors.

Finally, the doors open to what sounds like a pressure air release. Lights turn on in succession down three long aisles inside the chamber with pallets of Xerion stacked 100 feet high on each side of each aisle. Each aisle is 20 feet wide. The Treasury Chamber is immense.

Zeina, Jensen, Alex, and Reins are standing inside looking at the Xerion in awe. Jensen says, "There's enough Xerion here to fuel the entire Orion fleet for 1,000 years."

Suddenly, they hear enormous footsteps. It sounds like it's coming down an adjacent corridor crisscrossing the aisles at their mid-point.

"Squuaaaaakkkk" .... a horrible loud screeching sound rings throughout the chamber.

"What the hell is that?" hollers Alex.

They all draw their blades and stand behind Zeina who unfurls her glowing sword to point it in the direction from where the noise came.

It's turning the corner of the center aisle to come at them! Horror of horrors – it's a giant chimera creature!

Zeina screams,

"It's a Griffin! ... Everyone ... throw down your weapons!"

It's a giant Lion with the head, front feet, and wings of an Eagle. It's fierce and terrifying looking. It's furious. It charges up the aisle and in one fell swoop of its front right foot sends the whole Alpha team flying. They all slam up against the wall. The Griffin steps on Jensen's body and pierces his right shoulder with a giant talon while it grabs hold of Rein's battle suit with its mouth and tears the suit off of Rein's body. Zeina pulls on the Griffin's tail so it will stop attacking Jensen and Rein. The Griffin spins around and hits Zeina with its front left foot sending her flying across the room.

In the midst of the commotion, the music of a magic flute begins playing from a distance down one of the aisles. The Griffin hears the flute and halts its attack as the music grows increasingly louder. Walking up the aisle playing the magic flute is a small old man with long white hair (of the Castor clan) in a long white tunic. The Griffin's whole demeanor changes. It is delighted to see the old man. The old man pets the Griffin. The Griffin steps backward from Zeina and her team while nodding its head.

"Didn't you know you needed to come and see me before entering the Treasury Chamber? If I thought you were thieves, I would have allowed the Griffin to kill all of you!" says the old man.

"Sir, thank you for coming. We were not aware that a Griffin protected the treasury. I am Commander Zeina Bellatrix of the Orion Empire. We came to secure the Xerion, not to steal it. We will be moving it to a new secure location. You are welcome to join us."

"Your Highness, the honor is all mine. I am *Mr. Rourke*. I will help you move and secure the Xerion. The Griffin and I are its sworn guardians. Therefore, we will go wherever it goes," says Mr. Rourke.

"Lord Raiden and the ninth fleet are on their way here. They will transport the Xerion treasure to a secure location. You and the Griffin can travel with the Xerion to guard it at its new location," says Zeina.

CHAPTER THREE

FIERY ANGELS RISE

T he Betelgeuse and the Orion ninth fleet are approaching the
Constellation of Lupus on their way to the Trex star system.
Lord Raiden Bellatrix is standing alone with his hands behind
his back at the front of the Betelgeuse bridge watching the stars race by.
He's standing below the famous viewscreen dome arcing over the entire
bridge of the ship. The viewscreen dome turns straight down at the front
and returns inward at the floor to form the first section of the bridge
where he's standing. Standing there makes you feel as if you are flying
through space without the ship. It's Raiden's favorite place to stand.
The viewscreen is made of the same material as the ship's hull but
Orion technology allows it to turn translucent and operate interactively.

"Maia, drop the ninth fleet out of warp here in the Ursa-Indres.
Position the fleet in orbit around its largest gas giant, Typhon-Bose.
The fleet can cloak inside its powerful magnetic field," says Raiden.

Raiden prefers natural human interactions, such as speaking his
orders, rather than just making commands via the Com. This encourages
better ideas from other officers before a new course is implemented.

The fleet is now cruising together through the Ursa-Indres star
system approaching Typhon-Bose, a bright red gas giant five times the
size of Jupiter. Ursa-Indres is the closest star to the Trex star system.

"Ben, General Urlex and the Scorpion fleet are massing their
forces inside the Ackler Nebula just outside the Trex star system.
They're not going to let us take the Xerion without a fight even though
the Xerion technically belongs to the Orion Empire.

"What do you think, Ben? Do we attack first, or do we let them make the first move?" asks Raiden as he paces the bridge.

Lieutenant Ben Lor, an eight-foot red-haired giant from Aldebaran in charge of weapons and tactical, answers back,

"Sir, I suggest splitting the ninth fleet. Take half the fleet to form a blockade around M-Trex 3 to give our cargo ships the protection they need to teleport the Xerion. Keep the Betelgeuse and the rest of the fleet in Ursa-Indres around Typhon-Bose. When General Urlex moves in with the Scorpion fleet, then we attack from astern."

"Good plan, Ben. Let's make it so," orders Raiden.

Meanwhile, inside the Ackler Nebula, General Cyrus Urlex is sitting in the captain's chair of the new Scorpion flagship, the Antares, arguably the most powerful and menacing starship in the galaxy.

"Garrett, how much longer until all the Scorpion ships are in position inside the nebula?" asks Cyrus.

"Sir, the fleet is ready. We're just waiting for the Scorpion Core of Engineers to finish their work," answers Commander Garrett Cartrite.

Cyrus is visibly annoyed with the speed of the Core of Engineers. With a flustered face, he slams his armchair and says,

"What do I have to do, go down there and do the damn work myself? Who do we have down there, a bunch of imbeciles?"

Cyrus hits the intercom on his side console while shaking his head.

"Captain Kalek, what is taking you and your team so long?" asks General Urlex in an irritated tone.

"Sorry, Sir. All of the equipment is in place, connected, and functioning. The generators are running through their protocols to enter harmonic resonance with each core," answers Captain Kalek.

"How much time until they can be activated?" asks Cyrus.
"Nineteen minutes and 35 seconds, Sir," answers Kalek.

"Good! Do not activate until I give you the order myself. Do you understand?" asks Cyrus in his typical harsh tone.

"Aye, Sir, I understand completely," answers Kalek.
Cyrus cuts the intercom with Captain Kalek and looks over to Commander Garrett Cartrite standing nearby at a console and asks,

"Garrett, what is the position of the Orion cargo freighters?"

"There are now three Orion freighters parked in lunar synchronous orbit with the Bairus moon, the third moon of M-Trex 3. A third ship just joined the other two moments ago. The cargo ships are protected by the same small fleet of Orion military ships whose commando team is currently on the surface of M-Trex 3," answers Garrett.

"How many life signs are on those three cargo ships?" asks Cyrus.
"There are 231 life signs among the three ships," answers Garrett.

"Garrett, the moment you detect any teleport activity between the three cargo ships and the Xerion on M-Trex 3, tell me," orders Cyrus.

Back on the surface of M-Trex 3, Zeina is in the Treasury Chamber with a few more Orion officers who just arrived from the three cargo ships in orbit alongside the Bairus moon. The officers are attaching teleport transponders to all the pallets of Xerion to create a more powerful signal between the ships and the Xerion.

Using the Com, Zeina connects with a different Orion Commando team on the other side of M-Trex 3 who just commandeered and secured a second mining facility on the other side of the planet.

"Captain Liu, are you ready for teleport?" asks Zeina.
"Yes, Commander, we are ready to energize at your command," answers Captain Liu.

"Captain Liu, you are cleared to begin teleporting," says Zeina.
"Yes, Commander," answers the captain.

Meanwhile, half of the Orion fleet is arriving around M-Trex 3 to form a blockade. They're creating a ring around the entire system enveloping the planet and its three moons. One hundred massive black diamond Rigel Class 3 Destroyers are lining up around the system. Hundreds of other Orion ships are lining up between the Destroyers.

Back on the Antares, Garrett is at a logistics console.

"General, teleportation activity has just been detected on M-Trex 3. The teleport signal is being scrambled so we cannot pinpoint from where on the planet, but it's large. We're also detecting simultaneous teleport activity among the three Orion cargo ships most likely receiving the cargo. And that's not all, Sir. Hundreds of Orion military vessels are now dropping out of warp around M-Trex 3 to form a perimeter around the entire system including the three moons." reports Garrett.

Just as Garrett is finished reporting this information, Cyrus looks down to read on his console that the equipment he had the Scorpion Core of Engineers working on is ready for activation.

"Garrett, timing is everything. I need a better read on the size of the teleports between M-Trex 3 and the cargo ships. I want to make sure they have everything before we make our next move," says Cyrus.

"Aye, Sir, we're redirecting power and making adjustments to the field array to get a better read on the transmissions and weights.

"Sir, in the last few minutes, the cargo ships received more than 1,000 kiratons of material. That sounds like most of it based on what we know was down there," says Garrett.

"Very well!" exclaims Cyrus as he hits the intercom and says, "Captain Kalek, activate the generators!"

Suddenly, forcefields begin rising up from deep inside the three moons and M-Trex 3 to engulf the four bodies inside four separate forcefields. The three Orion cargo ships are now captured inside the Bairus moon forcefield.

"Scorpion fleet, this is General Cyrus Urlex. Attack the Orion fleet!" commands the General.

All the Scorpion ships inside the Ackler Nebula immediately jump into hyperspace. Moments later they're reappearing around M-Trex 3. As they emerge out of hyperspace, they're attacking the Orion fleet.

All the ships on both sides are ablaze with laser fire and torpedoes. It's a massive conflagration of explosions and ships on fire.

Dozens of scorpion assault ships are attacking one of the Orion destroyers. The destroyer's shields are holding but slowly losing power. A group of Orion fighter craft swarm up over top one of the large Scorpion ships and begin diving in together toward the ship in a V configuration. They fire to a point right in front of the ships where their laser fire converges into one super-powerful laser beam directed at the scorpion ship. The scorpion ship explodes as they pass through it.

On the Antares, General Urlex in the captain's chair commands, "Target the Lead Destroyer... Fire now!"

The Antares unleashes a super powerful laser cannon blast. Everyone aboard all the ships in the battle hears and feels a tremendous high-voltage wave running through and rattling their ships.

All the Orion crew members are stunned at what it could be. They look out their windows to see the massive neon blue Antares ship firing upon the Orion Destroyer, the *Theta-Orionis.* The Destroyer's shields are holding, but with just one shot it lost half its strength.

The Betelgeuse and the rest of the Orion fleet jump out of warp and immediately enter the fight.

"Target the Antares with everything we got and immediately teleport all crew members from the Theta-Orionis to the Betelgeuse." commands Lord Raiden.

Lieutenant Ben Lor launches a barrage of high-yield *Quisernetic Torpedoes* at the Antares while the other Orion ships are firing lasers.

The Antares is shaking with thunderous jolts as the quisernetic torpedoes pound the ship. Bodies are flying across the bridge. Red lights are blinking. Smoke is moving through the ship.

"Sir, we have casualties on decks 8, 9, and 10. We will not be able to take another blow like that!" warns Garrett.

"Garrett, target the Lead Destroyer. FIRE, NOW!" orders Cyrus.

The Antares opens fire on the Theta-Orionis. Again, there is a massive high-voltage buzzing sound rattling all the ships in the area. The Theta-Orionis Destroyer explodes into millions of pieces.

It's the first time an Orion Destroyer has ever been destroyed. Raiden stays focused. "BEN...FIRE AGAIN!" commands Raiden. The Betelgeuse fires another barrage of torpedoes at the Antares.

Cyrus yells, "COUNTERMEASURES!" as he sinks in his chair.

Large plates of the Antares detach from the hull of the ship moving outward into space to absorb the incoming torpedoes. The Antares is shaking violently while the countermeasures absorb the bombardment.

The Antares hails the Betelgeuse. Lord Raiden answers the call. General Urlex appears large on the Betelgeuse viewscreen.

"Raiden, I can do this all day! Do you want me to destroy a few more of your Destroyers? I will give you only one chance to save the lives of your crew. I have taken your commando team on the surface and your three cargo ships hostage. They all belong to me now. They're locked inside my forcefields. There is no way for you to take down these forcefields before losing several more of your Destroyers.

"However, I will make a trade with you. I will give you the Orion crew members on the surface in exchange for the three cargo ships full of Xerion. You have only one minute to decide," says General Urlex.

Raiden raises his hand to Maia to cut the viewscreen transmission. Raiden is now walking calmly back and forth on the bridge with his hand on his chin thinking about the next move.

Raiden raises his hand again to Maia to bring back General Urlex. The General appears large on the Betelgeuse viewscreen.

"Well, Raiden, what did you decide?" asks Urlex.

"General, why don't we do this. Technically, all the Xerion belongs to the Orion Empire, and you know this. M-Trex 3 is also an Orion-protected territory that has been under a treaty between the Dura and the Castors for the past 300 years, and you also know this. However, as an olive branch of peace, and to prevent any more casualties on both sides, we would be willing to accept the following,

"We will give you one cargo ship of Xerion, and in return, you will allow the safe passage of the Orion crews on M-Trex 3 and the three cargo ships. The cargo aboard the other two ships is ours," says Raiden.

The General stares at Raiden for a second and then shakes his head. "Commander Cartrite, detonate the atomics now," says Urlex.

Down on the surface of M-Trex 3, a blinding flash of light rushes across the planet from a massive explosion. A huge mushroom cloud is now rising high into the atmosphere.

Raiden is dazed staring down at the planet in disbelief. General Cyrus Urlex begins talking again,

"Raiden, at the same time you had special forces on the ground, so did we. We've been secretly planting atomics all around M-Trex 3 for the past three months. That was the *Ognu Power Station* and its surrounding villages I just destroyed. Your mining facilities will be down for many months. Ignis-7 and your beloved Orion crew are next. Now give me what I want!" demands Cyrus as he pounds his chair!

Raiden is beet-red and visibly furious, but he holds back his anger. He speaks silently on the Orion Com to Lieutenant Maia Elsu in charge of navigation. General Urlex cannot hear them.

"Maia, the Jinas system cannot lock onto our team?"

Maia answers, "No, Sir, the Omicron shielding is self-modulating and too powerful. I've never seen a shield this powerful before."

Raiden looks back at Cyrus and says, "Cyrus, you're a sick psychopath! But you win the day! Drop the shields and allow me to take my people, and you can have the three cargo ships of Xerion."

Cyrus nods in agreement and is moving his hand on his console.

"Raiden, I'm not dropping the shields, but I am lowering the power to allow you to lock onto organic matter such as your people. You will not be able to teleport heavy metals such as the Xerion. You will have only two minutes starting now," says General Urlex.

Raiden looks over at Maia and nods his head to proceed.

Maia and her team immediately begin locking onto the Orion crew aboard the three ships and down on the surface. The 231 crew members on the three cargo ships are safely teleported to the Betelgeuse as well as Zeina and the commando teams on the planet's surface. Raiden is also taking the opportunity to teleport various other Caster personnel who have been loyal to the Orion Empire.

"Raiden, we have everyone including the entire crew from the Theta-Orionis, the crew from the three cargo ships, Zeina and her whole team, and a few others," says Maia.

"Maia, direct the entire ninth fleet to the Aldebaran system, maximum warp," says Raiden.

A moment later, Maia says, "Raiden, Aldebaran is locked in."
"Excellent, Maia! … Engage!" says Raiden.

The Betelgeuse and the entire ninth fleet vanish into hyperspace on their way to the Aldebaran system.

Now that the fleet is moving at warp out of harm's way, Raiden begins to think about and digest everything that had just transpired.

"Ben, how many casualties did we suffer today?" asks Raiden.

"Sir, of the 300,000 plus officers we have serving in the ninth fleet, we lost 19 today, but we saved over 4,000," answers Ben.

"That's 19 too many, Ben, and how about the Ognu Power Station and all the innocent villagers!" says Raiden, shaking his head in disgust.

"Maia, how long until we arrive in Aldebaran?" asks Raiden.
"Six hours and 14 minutes, Sir," answers Maia.

Raiden sits down in the captain's chair and hits the ship-wide intercom and says,

"All senior officers, report to Assembly Hall One in one hour."

"Ben and Maia, please gather Royce and Kurzon and let's go greet my cousin Zeina down in Cargo Bay Six," says Raiden.

While walking, Raiden, Maia, and Ben meet Royce and Kurzon at one of the Jeffrey tubes. It will take them to Cargo Bay Six.

"Ah, Kurzon and Royce. Great to see you both! Kurzon, how are all our wounded?" asks Raiden.

"A few scrapes and bruises and a couple of broken bones, Raiden. Nothing serious. I thought it was about to get much worse. Thankfully, we saved the Theta-Orionis crew," says Kurzon, the ship's doctor.

"Royce, how's the ship?" asks Raiden.

"The ship functioned as expected and has some minor damage to the hull, but those repairs are moving along quickly. I am concerned about our next encounter with the Antares. We need to make some upgrades," says Royce, the Chief Engineer and an Artificial Human (Android).

"Agreed, Royce. Please prepare a list of your ideas for the upgrades and let's discuss as soon as you're ready," says Raiden.

They arrive at Cargo Bay Six. The door opens.

Standing there is Zeina and the commandos of the Alpha, Delta, and Gamma teams, as well as Captain Liu and his Epsilon team, and last but not least, the old man, Mr. Rourke, from the Treasury Chamber.

Maia and Ben are stunned to see what is stacked up beyond! Pallets of Xerion! The massive docking bay is full of Xerion!

Raiden is all smiles as he walks up to Zeina.

"Zeina, well done! Once again, you and your team saved the day!" exclaims Raiden as he expresses his satisfaction.

Zeina is very gracious. While smiling, she points to her team. "Raiden, meet the finest officers I've ever worked with!" says Zeina.

All the officers are lined up in uniform being greeted by Raiden. For most of them, it's the first time they're meeting Raiden or any member of the royal family. Raiden thanks each of them personally.

"Raiden, I also want you to meet Mr. Rourke. He saved us all from the giant Griffin," says Zeina as she brings the old man forward.

Mr. Rourke, the old man, bows up and down to Raiden with big smiles in his white tunic and sandals. Raiden smiles while placing one hand on the old man's shoulder and says, "Mr. Rourke, thank you so much for saving everyone! You will be rewarded! Where's the Griffin?"

Zeina answers for him and says,

"Oh, he's in Cargo Bay Seven. We will take you to see him."

After some more pleasantries, talking, and laughing with the team, Raiden walks over to Zeina and says,

"Zeina, can we step away from the others for a minute?"

She begins stepping away and says, "Sure, what's on your mind?"

They walk away quietly from the others. Raiden stops at the pallets of Xerion and looks at Zeina with a serious look in his eyes, and says, "Zeina, me, my father, Giao, and your dad are all so proud of you! Not just with your remarkable combat abilities, but your leadership, how you pull everyone together, how you function under pressure, your understanding of the human condition, your loyalty to the Orion Empire and everything we cherish and believe in.

"We formally ask if you would accept the official royal appointment of becoming the new Captain of the Betelgeuse?"

Zeina is truly surprised and says,

"What, the Betelgeuse? But I'm a field commander. I've never run a ship before!"

She's saying this while thinking about it. Raiden responds, "Zeina, you have all the instincts and skills to be a great ship captain. We need your leadership right now! We're at war with the Omicron.

Zeina turns and looks at Raiden and says, "Okay, I accept!"

Raiden is delighted and responds,

"I called a senior officer meeting in 30 minutes where I will announce your appointment! One of the first things you will need to do is pick your First Officer."

"How about the rest of my team?" asks Zeina.

"I will leave them to you. You decide where they all go next. Perhaps some of them should serve with you on the Betelgeuse," says Raiden.

As Raiden and Zeina are walking back to the team, Maia says, "Raiden, please explain how we got all this Xerion? Is this all of it?

"Maia, General Urlex got a pile of rocks. We got all the Xerion. What you see is only ten percent of it. Zeina and Royce redirected the Xerion to the cargo bays of 20 different Orion vessels. The three cargo freighters near the Bairus moon received slabs of granite and marble from Captain Liu's team who commandeered a second mining facility on M-Trex 3. The first rule of Orion command is *misdirection*.

"We can make a course of action look absolutely certain all the while doing something completely different," explains Raiden.

"But why then did you try to bargain for the Bairus moon cargo freighters?" asks Maia.

"If I didn't attempt to bargain for the freighters, Urlex would have become suspicious, possibly thinking, why is he giving up the freighters so easily? For misdirection to work, part of you has to believe in the ploy and act accordingly. Otherwise, it won't look authentic and someone like Urlex will smell it a mile away. That's also why I kept most everyone else in the dark. I needed you all to play the part," explains Raiden.

"Ah! Brilliant! Oh my God! Cyrus is going to go nuts! I wish we could see his face when he realizes it's only marble!

"Well, at least he can get a few new countertops out of it!" exclaims Raiden with a smile.

"Why are we taking the Xerion to the Aldebaran system and not Bellatrix?" asks Maia.

"We have thousands of such treasuries spread throughout the Milky Way Galaxy. Bellatrix already has hundreds of times what was on M-Trex 3. The Treasury on Karnox has capacity and our ships could use the fuel. Being the central command of the Orion Military, it's also the most fortified and protected planet in the galaxy," says Raiden.

They left Cargo Bay Six and stopped at Cargo Bay Seven to see the Griffin who was much friendlier to everyone this time. Lord Raiden was utterly enthralled by him, vowing that the giant Griffin would be revered and protected by the Orion Empire. Later that day, Zeina became the Captain of the Betelgeuse. Her appointment was met with thunderous applause by all the senior officers of the Betelgeuse. Zeina appointed Ben Lor as her new First Officer and Captain Sarah Marco of the Delta team as the new Lieutenant for Weapons and Tactical.

CHAPTER FOUR

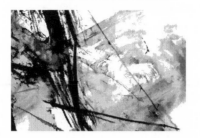

DARK SIDE OF THE MOON

Six months earlier, at the same time Lord Raiden Bellatrix was leaving his Orion home-world of Planet Erawan on the Daedalus to join the Betelgeuse in the Helix Nebula, Lord Giao Setairius, the older brother of Lord Raiden Bellatrix, began investigating the ancient religions of the galaxy. He was curious to see if he could find any references to a creation deity associated with the essence of matter.

Before using the cortical node again to enter the Omicron virtual reality construct known as the *Grid*, he was conducting as much research as possible. Was the supernatural deity he met on the Grid known as the *Gorgon,* just an elaborate AI, or was she something more? Also, was there any truth behind what the Gorgon had told him about his mother? If there was any truth behind what the Gorgon had told Lord Giao, he needed to find out for sure.

To read and study the most ancient texts, a person couldn't find the information on a computer. Long ago, it was considered sacrilegious by the ancient priesthood to store, share, and transmit the material via computers. This was to prevent the potential perversion of the texts.

The most ancient texts were found only in print and published only by the priesthood itself. The Orion Empire respected the old priesthood, and because of this, even thousands of years later, the manuscripts could still only be found in print. The best and most reliable sources of print were held in ancient buildings built by the priesthood. Scholars were allowed to visit and study inside these ancient buildings, but only with the strictest security measures and environmental controls to preserve the old manuscripts. With such limitations on the material, it was no wonder that knowledge of the ancient religions was limited.

"Raiden, I agree with you needing to be there, but I also urge you to stick to your plan. I see no reason to change it yet," says Lord Giao while talking to Lord Raiden on a mobile link.

Lord Giao ends his call with Lord Raiden to continue reading a book while in his chambers at the Orion Ministry on Planet Erawan.

The Orion Ministry was the building on Erawan where the official matters of the Monarchy were commonly managed, including that of the Orion Supreme Court, of which, Lord Giao was the Chief Justice. In the Orion Constitution, the Supreme Court was not a function of government; it was a function of the Monarchy. The lower courts, however, were considered a function of government. Government was beneath the Monarchy with no government buildings on Planet Erawan. All official government buildings were on Planet Olympia.

The Orion Ministry was only a short distance from the Royal Villa, the official residence of the royal family. The Orion Ministry building was made of solid white granite. Massive pillars of stone surrounded the building supporting a pyramid-shaped roof. The building emerged from a side of a mountain whose peak disappeared into a white fog. The truth is, there was no peak. The mountain disappeared beyond the sky into the crust of the planet itself. The Orion lived inside the planet.

One of Giao's court assistants walks into his mahogany wood chambers to find Giao looking down reading intensely at his desk.

"Sir, you called?" asks the assistant.

Giao is fixated on his book but then looks up to see the assistant. "Yes, please cancel all my appointments and reschedule all my court hearings for the week. I have an urgent matter to attend to," answers Giao.

Giao stands up from his desk, walks out of his chambers and down the hall to see his father, King Sah. The King is in his official chambers sitting next to his desk in front of an easel painting an oil painting.

"Yes, Giao, what can I do for you?" asks the King as he jabbers away at a canvas with his paintbrush.

"Father, I would like to receive your official permission to visit the sacred moon of Barstow. I wish to read from the ancient religious texts in the old Visndorf Cathedral on the dark side of the moon," says Giao.

The request quickly gets the King's attention as he places his paintbrush down and turns toward Giao with a pleased but inquisitive look.

"One of my favorite subjects! Why the sudden interest in the ancient mystery religions, Giao?" asks King Sah.

"I had a strange dream. It spurred my interest in ancient mythology and religious iconography. I would like to study what the old books had to say. Perhaps it will help me to decipher my dream," answers Giao.

"What was the dream about, if you don't mind me asking?" inquires King Sah with an interested look on his face.

"It was a dream full of symbols of nature, feminine iconography, the struggle between light and darkness, and perhaps an answer to the meaning of my life," answers Giao.

As Giao explained his dream, the King was looking down, listening intensely, nodding his head. Most importantly in the King's mind, however, is that he saw an opportunity to mend his relationship with his son through a shared interest in the ancient mystery religions.

"Ah...I understand. I authorize your trip. But remember, Giao. Barstow and Jenesis are forbidden worlds. There's a good reason why only I have the authority to grant access to Erawan's two sacred moons. They're forbidden to protect the extremely rare primordial descendent creatures remaining on them. We believe they're hyperdimensional.

"This is why the ancient priesthood built the Visndorf Cathedral on the dark side of the moon at the edge of light and darkness where many of these primordial creatures live and thrive until this very day. The Visndorf Cathedral at the top of Visndorf Mountain exists in a perpetual state of twilight due to its near polar location and the odd relationships between Barstow, Jenesis, Erawan, and the Bellatrix star," explains King Sah.

"I understand completely, father. As required, I will not be taking any technology to the surface other than my reading glasses so they can translate the ancient texts for me," says Giao.

"Very well, Gaio. I will let the custodian scientists and caretakers on the surface of Barstow know that you will be visiting to conduct your research. It's your first time going. Your brother Raiden hasn't been there yet either. Having no technology on the surface means you will be trekking up the mountain. It's actually been several years since my last visit. Enjoy, Giao," says King Sah.

A couple of hours later, Giao is home at the Royal Villa standing alone outside on the plaza near the lake waiting for a shuttle to take him off-world. A shuttle approaches in the sunlight creating sunbeams around the shuttle as it lands in front of him.

Giao walks up the ramp into the shuttle holding a small backpack around his right shoulder.

"Your Majesty, welcome aboard," says the pilot.

"Thank you, Hal. It's good to see you again," says Giao.

The shuttle lifts off quietly and is gliding just above the lake water. Birds on either side are racing the shuttle as Giao watches with a smile. The shuttle arcs to the right past a waterfall into a green canyon ravine. They're following the ravine when it opens into a big valley below with rolling green hills. They fly over the hills and arc straight up into a dark circular opening in the blue sky above surrounded by white puffy clouds.

They're moving through a dark void when suddenly it's full of city lights from super-tall towers elegantly machined out of solid granite. Small ships are flying back and forth blinking in a myriad of colors. They're flying freely among the buildings, dipping, rising, and weaving. The shuttle turns left and heads down a dark passage with an opening at the far end gleaming with sunlight. They emerge from the crevice of a rocky cliff into the blue Erawan atmosphere. Below them, the surface of the planet is full of soft pink and lavender colors, green foliage, and a large body of blue water beyond. Giao is admiring Erawan's pristine natural world when the shuttle suddenly rises swiftly into the blackness of outer space. Planet Erawan is now behind them glowing as a bright marble sphere of pastel colors floating amongst the stars.

They're approaching a large titanium-colored space station with dozens of small craft coming and going. It has a cylindrical midsection in the shape of a wide column with a large cantilevered dome on top. The midsection flows downward into a circular cone pyramid bottom. For security reasons, everyone changes shuttles at this planetary stargate, including the Royal Family. The Erawan stargate is a city unto itself. The people of Erawan call it, *Sky City*. It has everything a thriving metropolis would have. Giao and his crew exit the Erawan shuttle and walk to an interplanetary craft waiting to take them to the Barstow moon.

Giao and the pilot, Hal, are walking up to the Barstow shuttle craft. Standing in front of the shuttle are two women and two men. As they approach, the four give a courtesy bow to Lord Giao and Hal.

Hal nods to the four and points his hand toward Giao and says,

"Ladies and Gentlemen, I give you His Majesty, Chief Justice Lord Giao Setarious."

Giao responds and says,

"Please, everyone, just call me Giao. This is an unofficial visit. I hope we can all be friends on this trip."

One of the two women steps forward and says,

"Giao, please allow me to introduce myself. I'm *Doctor Annabel Stein*, the Chief scientist on Barstow. My friends call me Ann."

Giao gives Ann a courtesy nod.

"Giao, please allow me to introduce you to my colleagues *Hector, Jada,* and *Cisco*. Hector works with me on the science team. Cisco and Jada know a lot of the science but are technically *Trackers* with a good handle of the terrain on Barstow," says Ann.

"Excellent, I am very pleased to meet you all," says Giao, as he gives each of them a courtesy nod.

Hal, one of the commissioned pilots serving the Royal Family, relieves the Barstow shuttle pilot of his command so he can take over. Lord Giao's security detail performs a quick scan of the shuttle before he and the crew board.

The shuttle is cleared; the team boards and sits down together in the rear of the vessel on large cushioned chairs. The chairs pivot around so they can each face one another.

"Giao, we have been asked to escort you to the Visndorf Cathedral on the dark side of the moon. Is this still the plan?" asks Cisco while sitting down in his chair.

"Yes, Cisco, this is still the plan. I will be studying the ancient manuscripts preserved inside the Cathedral library," says Giao.

Ann, Cisco, Jada, and Hector look at each other for a second with an expression of concern. Ann jumps into the conversation with a smile,

"Giao, how much do you know about the Barstow moon, its environment, and the Visndorf Cathedral?" asks Ann.

Giao says, "Not too much, Ann. Even members of the royal family have limited knowledge of Erawan's two sacred moons. My father knows more than he will tell. He prefers to speak of it only with people who have been there. I don't understand all the suspense and mystery about it. Okay, fine, it has special life forms. But why all the secrecy?"

The four are looking at each other again at a loss for words.

"I agree with your father, Giao. I think it's best that people go there first, and then it's easier to discuss," says Ann.

Lord Giao is intrigued by Ann's agreement with his father. The shuttle is lifting off to glide out of the docking bay into space as they all look out the windows.

The shuttle craft arcs back around the space station as it circles Planet Erawan. They're hugging the planet, gliding above its clouds in space, when Jenesis, the twin moon of Barstow, appears at a distance. Shining with swirls of green, aqua, and white, Jenesis is growing larger and larger in the front viewscreen as they head toward the lunar world.

Jenesis is much smaller than Erawan but has a dense atmosphere with a warm tropical ecosystem. The crew is all smiles as they get up close to the moon while skimming its upper atmosphere from space. This is the closest Giao has ever come to the Erawan moon.

The ship passes over Jenesis only to reveal its twin moon, Barstow, closing in ahead. Barstow is a rusty orange color with thin pink swirls. It has mountains and seas of water reflecting a liquid-copper appearance.

As they approach Barstow, there's an Orion science vessel in orbit. "That's our ship, the *Equinox*," says Jada.

The shuttle passes over the front bow of the Equinox to begin descending into the Barstow atmosphere. As they descend into the clouds, it's raining large drops of water against an eerie bright orange sky. They break through the cloud deck only to reveal a completely different world beneath the clouds. Looking up, it's now a blue sky with white clouds and an evergreen forest below with giant redwood trees.

"Wow! An evergreen forest with blue skies. I didn't expect to see this based on the color of the moon from space," says Giao.

"That's just one of the many anomalies, Giao, but one that we can explain. The moon appears rust-colored from space, not because of its surface, but because of the air in its upper atmosphere," says Hector.

"Please explain," says Giao as he looks back and forth between Hector and the windows.

"An indigenous microscopic organism on Barstow we call the *Bream* produces a chemical through its digestion process we call *BetaCyrine4*, or BC4. The rusty pink color in the atmosphere is due to the presence of BC4. It has some very interesting medicinal properties. However, its most odd and peculiar attribute is the tricks of light it plays. It creates a natural camouflaging effect. From space, Barstow looks like a desert planet, but it's actually a forest moon," explains Hector.

"Amazing! I wonder why I've never learned of this," says Giao.

"It's one of Barstow's many well-kept secrets," says Cisco.

"Why would the priesthood keep that a secret?" asks Giao.

"Perhaps to suppress interest and keep people away," says Ann.

"Hmmm," murmurs Giao with a perplexed expression on his face as he turns back to look out the window with his hand on his chin.

A dark shadow begins moving across the forest as the shuttle flies over the redwood treetops against the setting of the Bellatrix sun on the distant horizon. Planet Erawan lingers boldly in the sky in crescent form. Dark crimson paints the horizon to cast a dim reddish glow across the landscape. In actuality, neither the Bellatrix sun, nor the Barstow moon, are moving in the sky. What's moving to create the sun-setting effect is the shuttle. On Barstow, where it's dark, it's always dark. Where it's light, it's always light. Where it's twilight, it's always twilight. They're venturing into Barstow's perpetual twilight realm. The shuttle is now setting down on a landing platform among the giant trees.

"No technology is allowed beyond the landing station," says Cisco.

"That's okay, Cisco. I'm prepared for that. The only technology I have with me are my reading glasses," replies Giao.

"We will be riding Areions to the Visndorf Mountain Cathedral. It's about an hour's trek from here at the very edge of light and darkness," says Jada.

Areions were magnificent alien horses which lived on distant worlds but were later mythologized on Earth in ancient Greece.

It's still fairly light outside, but they're already at a position where Bellatrix is partially below the horizon casting a red glow in the air. They disembark the shuttle and make their way to a nearby horse stable.

Giao and the four are walking along a dirt pathway to the stables from the shuttle platform. Hal and the shuttle are lifting off behind them into the atmosphere and quickly vanish into the clouds. Large green vegetation lines both sides of the trail. Giao can hear the sound of a small brook of water flowing behind the shrubbery alongside the path. He also hears the light knocking of a piece of wood directing the flow of water. Suddenly, a little man, only about three feet tall, emerges from the brush holding a bucket of water. He stands before them on the path for only a second, looking up at them with a big smile, and then hustles off to the other side into the bushes.

"Wow! A little man. What was that? That was not a Cherub like we know on Erawan," says Giao.

"That, Giao, was an *Elf*. It's a hyperdimensional being. They live on both Barstow and Jenesis," answers Ann.

"What do you mean by hyperdimensional? My father used the same word. Are the Cherubs on Erawan hyperdimensional?" asks Giao.

"Hyperdimensionality is a spectrum. We say an object or life form is *On the Spectrum* when it's not completely here in our physical world. It phases in and out of our reality. We actually do believe that the Erawan Cherubs are on the spectrum, but they are closer in frequency to the rest of the life on Erawan, including the Erawan humanity, and therefore they are less anomalous. This is why some may not think of them as hyperdimensional," explains Ann.

"What is hyperspace? Is the hyperdimensional realm the Primordial Universe?" asks Giao.

Ann answers and explains, "Good questions, Giao.

"Hyperspace is not the same as the Primordial Universe. Hyperspace is still the Physical Universe, but just a higher frequency of the Physical Universe. Hyperspace is the hyper-physical. It exists on a perpendicular plane to our reality, just around the corner, out of sight. We have no idea of how or why it's there. We just know it's there.

"We still have a lot to learn about hyperspace. At the moment, we have more questions than answers. We are still amateurs when it comes to *Hyperspace Technology*. Technically, *Warp Drive* sinks a ship into hyperspace when it's traversing space-time, but we utilize it more than we actually understand it. The same can be said of *Fractal Resonance* technology allowing light to pass through solid matter. We utilize it. We know how to make it turn on and off. But we don't have a deep understanding of it yet.

"The Primordial Universe is something entirely different from hyperspace. The Primordial Universe is the mother-universe to the Physical Universe. We believe it exists behind the *Singularity Wall*. Everything in our physics models indicates it is there and we have historical documents describing the *Anthro-Orionis* and the legend that they descended from the Primordial Universe, but we have never actually detected it, and we have no physical Anthro-Orionis specimen. We have a working hypothesis of how it all comes to together, but again, we actually don't know.

Ann sees a straight tree branch lying across the path. She picks it up and starts using it as a walking stick and continues her explanation.

"We believe life crossed over from the Primordial Universe to the Physical Universe via the medium of water. More specifically, we believe life crossed over from the primordial to the physical via a body of water while that body of water was sunken inside hyperspace. The body of water needs to be high enough in the spectrum to allow for the crossing. On Jenesis and Barstow, we are closer to it," explains Ann.

"But how can a science team study this with no technology on the surface of the two moons?" asks Giao.

"Oh, we have technology," answers Hector, as he pulls a device out of his bag blinking with lights.

"You're allowed to carry only the essential technology needed for your purpose, like your reading glasses. The science team only carries the devices it needs to conduct its research," explains Hector.

"Okay, but why limit the technology?" asks Giao.

"Because as strange as it sounds, evidence indicates that the more synthetic technology exists within a hyperspatial realm, the more the vibrational speed of that realm slows and becomes more solid. We don't see it happening because we're a part of it, " answers Cisco.

"Hyperspace, vibrational resonance, organic life, is all interchangeable. The moment you start messing with it, trying to change it to create a technology, it starts to slow down and solidify. It's one of the many mysteries of hyperspace," explains Jada.

"So, what are you telling me? That Barstow and Jenesis, as entire worlds, exist on the spectrum, and that by limiting the technology on the surface of each world, we are somehow preserving their place within the spectrum?" asks Giao.

"Yes, that's exactly right, Giao. And to add to that, the reason we can see the hyperdimensional creatures so easily while on Barstow and Jenesis is because our own vibrational frequencies are increased while on the surface. All of us are a step higher in the spectrum right now. Barstow itself placed us there," says Ann.

Cisco has a smirk on his face and is visibly amused by something. Jada gives him an elbow.

"Speak up, Cisco. What's so funny?" asks Giao.

"Giao, what they're not telling you is that, not everything in hyperspace consists of innocent little elves and butterflies. There's some really scary stuff here, too!" says Cisco.

Giao just looks over at Cisco with one eyebrow raised. Just when Cisco says this, the group is arriving at the Areion horse stable. They walk inside the stables to see a group of large muscular black horses.

Areions have a few unique features differentiating them from all other horse breeds, including their large size, midnight blue eyes, and a pronounced curve in the back of their necks, giving their heads and neck a classic D shape. It's considered the King of Kings of horse breeds.

"Dad...look...It's Cisco! He's come back!" hollers Tim, a small boy running up to Cisco and the group. Mr. Fitz, a middle-aged man in overalls, walks out of one of the stalls.

"Cisco and Jada, welcome back! You brought friends! We don't get too many visitors! Very nice to meet you all," says Mr. Fitz.

"Mr. Fitz, it is my honor to introduce you and Tim to His Majesty, Lord Giao Setairius," replies Cisco, as he looks over at Giao.

Little Tim is paralyzed with his eyes and mouth wide open. Mr. Fitz politely steps up, bows, and begins speaking,

"Lord Giao, it is so very nice to meet you. Your father visited us several years ago. I've been hoping that one day we would meet some other members of the royal family. We are most honored by your visit. Our horses are well rested if you need them today."

"The honor is all mine, Mr. Fitz. Your hospitability is very much appreciated. Barstow is remarkable. I've only been here a few minutes and already I've seen wonders to boggle the mind," says Giao.

Giao kneels on one knee to talk to Tim and says,

"Tim, Cisco tells me what a great friend you are. I also hear that you are a great Checkers player. You and I will have to play a game when we come back from our trek up the mountain."

Little Tim is completely thrilled but keeps his composure and says,

"Yes, Mr. Giao, I mean, Your Majesty. I would love to play you a game of Checkers."

Giao pats Tim on his shoulder and stands up. Cisco speaks,

"Mr. Fitz, thank you so much for offering us the horses. We will need five horses for only two days."

"Just give us 30 minutes and we will have the horses ready for you. We know you will take good care of them. Which mountain will you be climbing if you don't mind me asking?" asks Mr. Fitz.

"Visndorf Mountain," chimes in Jada.

"Aha! Glad I asked. That rules out Jella and Nabi. They're both easily spooked. The last time Jella made the trip, she ran off. It took us hours to find her. And where did we find her? She was right back here in her stable. We will give you only our bravest horses," says Mr. Fitz.

Giao has a curious look on his face and asks the group,

"What's up with Visndorf Mountain? Every time it's mentioned, people have a strange reaction."

"Giao, on Barstow, especially where we're going, the mind tends to play tricks on people. Keep a positive mind by thinking positive thoughts, and everything will be just fine," says Ann.

"Yeah...that works until the first moment you get spooked and then it's all downhill from there," says Cisco sarcastically.

"Giao, hyperspace functions much like a mirror of the inner self. It's one of the many anomalies of hyperspace for which scientists still have a poor understanding," says Hector.

He then asks Giao, "Do you have bad dreams?"
Giao is amazed to hear scientists talking this way, but answers,

"No, actually, I normally sleep very well."
"Then you should have no problem," says Hector.

A short time later, everyone is outside the stalls getting mounted atop their horses. Mr. Fitz is helping Lord Giao who is already sitting on his horse. Mr. Fitz is checking the straps.

"Giao, we gave you our bravest horse. His name is Kelso. He's very protective and loyal. He will never leave you," says Mr. Fitz.

Giao is petting the horse, whispering in his ear. Kelso appears happy and excited for the pending trip and is responding well to him.

The group leaves the horse stable. The horses are trotting along a dirt road lined with tall smoldering fire lamps. Their scent fills the air.

Giao is riding between Ann and Cisco with Ann on the left and Cisco on the right. Jada and Hector are close behind riding side by side.

Strange ancient dark-colored trees with a thick wrinkled bark line the road. They're curving, bending, and twisting into the air.

Giao is staring at the trees. For a second, it looks as if one of the trees is moving its limbs in response to Giao looking at it. He shakes his head and refocuses on the road ahead.

Cisco begins talking, "Giao, in about a half-hour, we will reach the foothills of Visndorf Mountain. It will take another half-hour to reach the mountain's summit where on top is the ancient cathedral. The base of the cathedral has 100 steps. The horses will not be able to climb them. Everything inside the cathedral is carried up the steps by human hands.

"The priesthood did this to limit what could be brought in and out. We'll spend the next two nights in the cathedral to give you time for your research. No one in our group here has ever slept in the building before other than me. I once spent one night there," says Cisco.

As the group slowly trots along, the light of the Bellatrix sun grows dimmer, flooding the twilight air with an eerie crimson glow. The group is silent when suddenly they hear a high-pitched squawking sound in the distance. Jada and Cisco immediately look at each other with an expression of concern.

"What was that?" asks Giao, as he looks back and forth between Ann and Cisco for an answer.

That, Giao, was a *Sasquatch*. It's the Guardian of the Threshold of hyperdimensional space here on Barstow. Its job is to fight evil in the hyperdimensional realm. It protects the innocent and vulnerable creatures living in hyperspace from predators. The predators ultimately lower the vibrational resonance of the entire ecosystem," answers Cisco.

Ann decides to chime in, "In other words Giao, in temporal mechanics, the job of the Sasquatch is to help the entire planetary ecosystem maintain its place in the hyperdimensional spectrum."

Jada speaks up and adds to the discussion,

"He knows we are near, and he's letting us know that he knows we are near," says Jada.

Giao nods his head, signaling that he understands, but he is more interested in Kelso at the moment who seems to be observing something Giao and the others don't see. Kelso is snorting and grunting and wants to move faster.

Suddenly, a huge sasquatch charges out of the brush running across the road about 50 feet in front of them. It's a giant, hairy, humanoid being standing over ten feet tall. The creature is covered with shaggy brown hair from head to toe. Now standing in the road on the other side from which it came, it reaches into the shrubbery and pulls out by its neck a horrific-looking lizard-dog monster with glaring red eyes, two arms, two legs, a long tail, and spines running along its back.

The lizard monster is flailing its arms and legs, trying to bite the sasquatch. The sasquatch throws it down on the ground.

The lizard monster is now on all fours with its back hunched up, hissing a horrible noise. It has long fangs coming out of its mouth and massive talons on its feet. Its tongue is slithering in and out of its mouth.

A second sasquatch runs out of the brush, grabs hold of the lizard monster's tail, starts swinging it around, and then throws it against a tree. The first sasquatch picks up the lizard creature, breaks its back over his knee, and starts pounding its head with his foot, killing the monster.

The second sasquatch runs back into the brush while the first one stops for a second to look at Giao, Ann, and Cisco and then runs into the brush to follow the second sasquatch.

The whole team is paralyzed by what they just witnessed. Giao breaks the silence and says, "Ann, it doesn't seem safe out here. Should we go back?" Ann replies, "Giao, Barstow has its risks. However, I can tell you that my team and I have never been attacked by a predator before. The predators are typically more interested in small creatures. What we just witnessed, we have never seen before. The sasquatch was protecting us. If you wish to go back, we can."

Cisco pulls a long blade out of a pouch on his horse and says, "Giao, here, I have an extra blade if you wish to hang onto this."

Giao takes the blade.

"Well, that makes me feel a little better that we at least have some means of self-defense. Who else has a blade?" asks Giao.

All four pull out their blades and show them to him. "Aha, are you all trained to use your blades?" asks Giao.

"We all have combat and predator training, Giao. Especially Cisco and Jada," answers Hector.

"Giao, there are risks here, but in the ten years that I have been on Barstow, I have never been attacked by a predator. However, twice I stepped in to defend an elf. Predators prey on innocent and defenseless creatures. We are too large. We remind the predators of the sasquatch. That's why predators run from us. The elves call the sasquatch, *Yeti*, but we already use the word Yeti for something else," says Cisco.

"Understood, Cisco. Does anyone wish to go back?" asks Giao. No one raises their hand.

"Very well then. Let's proceed," says Giao. The horses continue forward. A moment later, Giao asks Ann,

"What was that lizard-dog creature? How does something so horrible even exist here on Barstow?

"We call it *Chupacabra*. Many of the creatures on Barstow manifest out of the *Noosphere*. Barstow's placement in hyperspace makes noosphere manifestations possible. Do you know what the noosphere is, Giao?"

"I've seen it mentioned a couple of times before. I believe it's what some call the planetary group mind. But that's all I know about it," answers Giao.

Ann continues,

"That's correct, Giao. The noosphere rises out of the collective effect of all the individual minds on a planet entering into resonance with one another via the host planet they all share. Every planet with life has its own noosphere. It affects all of us unconsciously, creating a self-reinforcing dynamic. What we feed into the noosphere cycles back into all the minds and all minds in turn cycle right back into the noosphere. Darkness begets more darkness. Light begets more light.

❖ CHAPTER FOUR ❖

"This is another reason Barstow and Jenesis are forbidden worlds. We need to limit the amount of darkness we introduce into the system. All human life has a dimension of darkness within it. If we introduce too much human life into the system, the entire system will become too heavy, and Barstow and Jenesis will fall out of hyperspace.

"Chupacabra is a manifestation of the darkness latent in the system. It manifests directly out of the noosphere. If Barstow were ever to fall out of hyperspace, the Chupacabra would no longer spontaneously manifest. However, the darkness would still be in the system and continue to affect all minds in its sphere of influence.

"The noosphere is a psychokinetic sphere instrumental to the evolution of life. Life on a planet naturally arises out of the noosphere."

Giao is amazed by all the information.

"Remarkable! I'm getting more than I bargained for on this trip. All I wanted to do was study an ancient manuscript, but I'm also getting a great education the higher worlds," says Giao.

"So far, sasquatch has done a good job maintaining the delicate balance in the ecosystem," says Jada.

"Along with a little help from us," remarks Hector.
"The biggest help from us has been to stay away," responds Jada.

Up ahead is a fork in the road.

"All, we need to take a right up ahead. The road to the right will take us to Visndorf Mountain," says Cisco.

They take the road to the right, which turns into an all-green heavily foliaged area, and enter into a passageway cut into the greenery. On the other side of the foliage is a river with a bridge made of stone and wood planks. The wood planking is turned up preventing passage.

"All, we need to wait for a moment at the entrance of the bridge," says Cisco.

After waiting for a couple of minutes, a little man, only about three feet tall with a long red beard and a funny sock-like brown hat, waddles out from underneath the bridge in brown overalls and approaches them. He walks up to Cisco with his hand out and says in a squeaky voice,

"One big coin for passage, please."

Cisco has the coin ready and places it in his hand. The little troll waddles over to the bridge and lowers the road. They cross the bridge.

CHAPTER FIVE

FLIGHT OF THE VALKYRIE

A week had passed since His Majesty's science team was first assembled deep beneath the Permian Ocean on Planet Artep. The twelve members of the scientific team, led by Qurel Song, visited the Permian anomaly multiple times to conduct as much study and analysis of the anomaly as possible. The entire team is still there. At this same moment, Lord Raiden Bellatrix and the new captain of the Betelgeuse, Captain Zeina Bellatrix, are on their way to the Aldebaran system to deliver the Xerion treasure they had secured from M-Trex 3.

Zeina is sitting in the center command chair on the Betelgeuse with Lord Raiden alongside on her right. He gave up the center chair so Zeina could start getting accustomed to being in command.

The viewscreen dome is in full transparent mode with all the stars approaching the front view of the ship to streak overhead into bright lines of light. Just as they're admiring the stars, Qurel Song materializes on the bridge of the ship at the very front walking towards Raiden and Zeina in the form of a holographic projection. He appears solid, like all the other crew members, but with a blue halo of light around him.

Qurel is actually still on Artep inside a holographic reflection chamber. The chamber replicates the environment of the Betelgeuse in real-time. Because the reflection chamber on Artep, and the Betelgeuse in space, are both Orion technologies controlled by the same Orion system, such a communication between the two locations is possible.

"Captain Zeina Bellatrix, congratulations. I cannot think of a better Orion officer to take command of the Betelgeuse," says Qurel as he gives her a respectful bow.

Zeina nods to Qurel in return with a smile. Qurel turns toward Raiden, bows, and says,

"Your Majesty, I have come to report our latest findings on Artep. It is most urgent."

Raiden immediately stands up and says,

"Qurel, Zeina, let's walk to the front to speak more privately." Qurel briefly nods at Ben, Maia, and the other officers of the bridge standing nearby and then follows Raiden and Zeina. They walk to the front of the ship where the three stop to stand on the transparent section of the bridge with the stars racing beneath their feet.

"What have we discovered?" asks Raiden with Zeina at his side.

"Sir, for the first time ever, we discovered one of the hyperspace portals spoken of in Anthro-Orionis lore," answers Qurel.

Raiden and Zeina are stunned with expressions of disbelief.

Qurel responds to their reactions by continuing,
"I know; it's incredible. However, we don't know yet where it leads or if we could get someone back if we sent them through."

"Have we sent a probe through?" asks Zeina.

"Yes, we have sent several, each with a different configuration. However, every time a probe enters the aperture and crosses the event horizon, we lose communication with it," answers Qurel.

"How is that possible, Qurel? We use quantum-based communications. Time and space should have no impact on the ability of the probe to signal back, even if it's on the other side of the universe. Distance and location should have no relevancy," argues Raiden.

This is true, Raiden, but remember, there are (1) things we know, (2) things we know we don't know, and (3) things we don't know we don't know. This could be a case of the latter. There could be a set of physics involved for which we have no knowledge, or the probes may have simply been destroyed. There are several different things which could be happening as the probes go through. We are eliminating the possibilities. But we do believe it is a hyperspace portal." says Qurel.

"So, what do you recommend we do next?" asks Raiden.

"The study group recommends we send a sentient being through the aperture. Not necessarily an organic human, but something that can respond intelligently on the other side and hopefully find its way back. We would need your permission," says Qurel.

"Who or what would you recommend sending through?" asks Raiden with his hand on his chin.

"We recommend sending an artificial humanoid being such as Royce, Euclid, or Axum. It's a very high risk for them. However, we could back up their mind, or their consciousness, so to speak. If they're destroyed, we can download their mind into a new android body.

Raiden responds, "It's against the law to back up the mind of a sentient living being, even if they agree to it, especially a senior Orion officer such as Royce. The mind could be stolen, exploited, and abused."

"I understand, Sir, that's why I am here," says Qurel. Raiden is looking at the stars while taking a moment to think about it. After a few seconds, he turns around toward Qurel and says,

"Under the circumstances, I will allow you to back up a sentient android mind. But this investigation is now strictly a military operation with the science academy in support, not in the lead.

"Zeina, with Ben Lor succeeding Qurel as the First Officer of the Betelgeuse, my father and I have elevated Qurel to Viceroy.

"Qurel now has the same level of authority as me for any posts he is appointed by the monarchy. As Viceroy, Qurel has been appointed Vice-Admiral of the Orion Ninth Fleet and Chancellor of the Pleiadean Science Academy." Zeina interjects and says,

"Qurel, if there is anyone outside the royal family who truly understands the monarchy and can speak on its behalf, it is you."

Qurel gives a courtesy nod to Zeina. Raiden continues,

"The Science Academy has never had or needed a Chancellor. Qurel will be the first. However, with the times we are in, my hope is he will bring a greater harmony and efficiency amongst its branches. We are at war. Any scientific breakthroughs made must be immediately studied for military application. I have always served as the Admiral of the Ninth Fleet and will continue to do so. However, by Qurel becoming the Vice-Admiral, this maintains all his security clearances and allows him to utilize all the resources of the Ninth Fleet.

"Chief Engineer Royce Allen is the best choice for this mission. However, Royce reports to Zeina on the Betelgeuse.

"Zeina, you now report to Qurel. The Betelgeuse will take charge of the research operation on Artep. As soon as we deliver the Xerion, we will go to Artep," says Raiden as he finishes giving his orders.

"Aye, Sir," says Qurel. "Aye, Sir," says Zeina.

Qurel walks in the direction of outer space and vanishes.

Raiden and Zeina remain standing at the front of the bridge.

Just as Qurel disappears, the Betelgeuse is arriving in the Aldebaran system, the headquarter star system of the Orion military. It's a giant stellar system with a massive orange central star 44 times the width of the Sun. It's been completely militarized over millions of years into a vast galactic fortress. The original humanity of Aldebaran began the militarization of the system. The Orion Empire completed it.

Thousands of massive sentient artificial machines, miles in size, work non-stop designing, fabricating, and building incredibly large celestial structures and starships. For millions of years, they have been working non-stop. The machines know how to harvest the star for all the elements they need. They don't harvest the planets, only the star.

Aldebaran has 20 orbiting planets, 15 of which are terrestrial-sized. Nine of the 15 terrestrial planets were moved in from other star systems and placed in orbit around Aldebaran. The first two of the 15 terrestrial planets, Liraset and Gem, are among the original Aldebaran planets and are conserved as natural worlds.

The other 13 terrestrial planets were augmented into planet-sized space stations. Twelve of the 13 space stations serve one of the 12 Orion fleets. The only space station not hosting a fleet is the central military headquarters known as Karnox. The 13 space stations were moved into close proximity of one another and aligned on the same side of the star. Karnox is at the center. It is number seven of 13.

On the other side of the star, 180 degrees apart from the string of space stations, exist the remaining seven planets of Aldebaran, including its original home-world, Liraset, its sister Gem, and five gas giants.

The planets on the Liraset side of the star were re-aligned with Liraset at the center. It's the fourth of seven. From above, the solar system looks like a propeller with Aldebaran as the center axis, the military side as one blade, and the Liraset side as the other blade. All the celestial bodies continuously orbit the star but stay in perpetual alignment.

Once a planet has been transformed into an artificial space station, the Orion no longer refer to it as a *Planet*. They call it a *Plexus*.

Karnox is the *Central Plexus*. The other twelve don't carry a name. All they have is a designation, i.e., Plexus 1, Plexus 2. The ninth plexus serves the ninth fleet. The tenth plexus serves the tenth fleet, and so on.

A vast network of glowing etheric ley lines connects each plexus to the central plexus to direct the flow of starships. From afar, it looks like a bundle of fiber optic cables strung among the cosmos with all the starships moving along the filaments pulsing like light beams in space.

When one of the fleets arrives around its host plexus, all the ships of that fleet enter into preset docking positions organized on a spherical honeycomb lattice structure encompassing the entire plexus. All the large destroyers and flagships line up along the equator interspaced by incredibly massive disc-shaped colony ships. While docked at a plexus, a colony ship functions as a city in space with a planet-like interior.

The sheer magnitude of the structure encapsulating a plexus is breathtaking and simply incredible. The surface world of a plexus is purely utilitarian serving the purpose of the plexus. However, Karnox hosts a massive underground city network of ten billion people who live and work inside the planet no different than any other planet.

The Betelgeuse drops out of warp. They're approaching the stellar defense grid encompassing the entire Aldebaran system. Before them is one of the stargates leading into the system.

Unlike the Bellatrix star system, craft of all sizes are allowed into the Aldebaran domain, but mostly only Orion military vessels. Starships belonging to a humanity outside of the Orion Empire are directed to the Liraset side of the star. Being the original home planet to the humanity of Aldebaran, Liraset is considered sacred and is officially recognized as such by the Orion Empire. In their ancient religion, the people of Liraset claim to be the original guardians of the galaxy.

The rest of the ninth fleet is dropping out of warp behind the Betelgeuse. The stargate takes hold of all the ships in the fleet and instantly knows everything about each ship, including each ship's docking position around the ninth plexus. The fleet begins flowing and streaming inward. As far as the ships are concerned, they've come home. When they reach the ninth plexus, each ship will receive a level of maintenance and upgrades they could only receive at the plexus.

The ninth plexus has taken hold of the Betelgeuse as it enters the stargate into the system. The network of cosmic ley lines is guiding it forward inside what looks like a tunnel of light. The ley lines are grouped on a cylindrical axis creating the tunnel-of-light effect.

They're cruising past massive stellar structures lining the cosmic highway system interconnecting each plexus. Millions of ships are passing back and forth on all sides of the Betelgeuse.

They're finally slowing down.

The tunnel of light has given way to a remarkable view of the ninth plexus. It's a luminescent neon blue sphere the size of a planet. The neon blue light is an atmosphere glowing from behind a giant honeycomb ship docking structure encapsulating the entire plexus. The number of ships deployed in a fleet is only a fraction of the total plexus capacity.

Raiden and Zeina are standing together at the front of the bridge while the Betelgeuse is approaching its enormous stellar docking bay.

Raiden says out loud,

"Royce, will you please come to the bridge."

The Orion Com instantly connects Raiden and Royce.

Royce hears Raiden via the Com inside his mind. Royce replies,

"Yes, Your Majesty. I will be right there."

A moment later, Royce enters the bridge walking up to Raiden and Zeina while the Betelgeuse is gliding into its docking bay.

Raiden looks over to Royce and says,

"Royce, thank you for joining us. We have an urgent matter."

Raiden looks upward and continues, "M, please download to Royce, all information regarding the operation on Artep involving the Permian Anomaly. Authorization, *Raiden, Echo Nine, Alpha Tango*."

Royce is standing motionless with a blank stare as he downloads all the information about the Permian Anomaly and its Orion discovery mission, *Ocean Horizon*. He's finished. He looks at Raiden and says,

"Fascinating! I take it that I am your choice to enter the aperture and that is why you have called me here?" Raiden replies,

"Yes, Royce, you are correct. It was not an easy decision to make. You are a sentient being and a core team member of the Betelgeuse. You have also become a friend. In your short time as an Orion officer, all of what you have accomplished is nothing short of extraordinary. But I must put the interests of humanity above both yours and mine.

"If this is actually what they say it is, we stand to make a huge leap forward. You are the most suited for the mission. It is a very high risk to you. If you would rather not take this risk, then I will choose another officer. The decision is yours. If you agree to the mission, I have already made a special exception and authorized that your mind be backed up in case you are killed entering the aperture."

Royce doesn't need long to think because he's an android. He's processing...processing...processing.

He stops, looks over at Raiden, and says,

"I accept the mission. I recognize the mission's value and its importance, and I agree, I am the best choice."

"Very well then. Zeina, Royce, please work together in developing a mission plan. All the information of the study group and all the resources of the Maricrisodon and Atlas are at your disposal. But before you begin, I have something to show you both," says Raiden.

Zeina and Royce look at Raiden with curious faces.

"Maia, please beam me, Zeina, and Royce to the Ninth Plexus at the coordinates I had previously shared with you," says Raiden.

"Aye, Sir, locking on and energizing now," says Maia.

Raiden, Zeina, and Royce disappear from the bridge of the Betelgeuse and re-materialize inside a room overlooking a docking bay. On the other side of a giant glass wall is a new starship hovering inside the docking bay with a person in a spacesuit moving along the exterior of the ship making a final inspection.

"Wow! Now that's a beautiful ship!" remarks Zeina as she stares at the starship. The starship is angular and stealthy looking with multiple intersecting planes peaking along its back like a spine spiking into the air in a black matte finish with no windows, inlets, or outlets.

Royce makes a calm matter-of-fact statement,

"Ah, yes, the new Valkyrie. A Runner Class Command ship just like your ship, the Daedalus, Your Majesty, but a whole new generation. It possesses the very latest in combat abilities, including hyperspace magnification otherwise known as *Cloaking*. Our engineers also managed to incorporate quisernetic torpedoes, which before the Valkyrie, could only be outfitted on large starships."

"Have we finally figured out how to submerge a ship inside hyperspace without having to teleport or go to warp?" asks Zeina.

"No, Zeina, that is still beyond our ability. As far as we know, only the Dominion have such knowledge and capability. Our cloaking technology merely magnifies hyperspace around the ship through the manipulation of gravity. The ship is still completely solid and physical. It's just hidden by a blanket of space. It cannot pass through matter and can still be hit by a weapon while cloaked," explains Royce.

Raiden interjects,

"You certainly know your hardware, Royce."

Raiden looks over at Zeina and says,

"Zeina, the Valkyrie is all yours. She will dock underneath the Betelgeuse just like the Daedalus."

Zeina is speechless and in awe as she looks back and forth between Raiden and the Valkyrie.

Raiden continues,

"She has a maximum crew capacity of 100, just like the Daedalus. This grants her access to the Bellatrix star system since nothing larger is allowed through. I was thinking she could make her maiden voyage today and take us to Artep. What do you both think?" asks Raiden.

"Let's do it! And thank you for entrusting me with another incredible ship. It will be another member of my crew," says Zeina.

"That she is Zeina. The Valkyrie is an extension of you, just like your sword. Urlex has no idea what is coming his way," says Raiden.

Royce chimes in,

"This is a good idea. The Betelgeuse needs to stay behind at the Ninth Plexus to undergo a series of new upgrades. We need to prepare for our next encounter with the Antares."

"Agreed, Royce. I hereby order that the entire Ninth Fleet undergo a complete reassessment with as many new upgrades as possible for doing battle with the new Scorpion Fleet," says Raiden.

"Sir, I would like to place Ben Lor in charge of the reassessment and upgrade program," says Zeina.

"Agreed, and so it is ordered," replies Raiden

"Your Majesty, in my absence, I request that Euclid work as second in command to Commander Ben Lor on the fleet upgrades. Euclid and I can process data together remotely. We can even utilize telemetric mirroring if needed. It will keep me in the loop while on Artep."

"Agreed, so it is ordered.

"Zeina, Royce, let's meet on the Valkyrie in two hours to go to Artep. In the meantime, both of you get with Ben and Maia and start developing a plan for the fleet upgrades.

"Royce, connect with Euclid and get him mobilized and debriefed. Zeina, coordinate with the Karnox Treasury Minister Elon Talex on transferring the Xerion from the Betelgeuse and the other ships of the fleet to the Treasury Chamber on Karnox," says Raiden.

"Will do, Sir.

"Minister Talex and I have already been coordinating. The Xerion is in the process of being offloaded and transferred via the proper chain of custody," says Zeina.

"Thank you, Zeina. I wish I could stay and see my son Oren today. He's on Karnox undergoing his cadet training and evaluation, but I need to be on Artep. I will come back and see him," remarks Raiden.

Zeina is sticking her head outside the door, waving at someone on the outside. A second later, Oren walks in behind Raiden who doesn't see him yet.

"Raiden, you shouldn't have to wait to see Oren," says Zeina. "Yeah, Dad, stop avoiding me; otherwise, I'm just going to have to take you down in the dojo," says Oren.

Raiden turns fast around and hollers, "Oren!" He gives Oren a big hug.

Raiden is laughing at Oren and Zeina and says, "Did you all conspire or what?"

Oren replies, "Dad, remember Zeina is my cousin. We do talk, you know!" as he continues amused.

Royce is watching with interest, trying to understand human emotion, which truly puzzles him, as it does most androids.

Zeina leans over and whispers to Royce that they should exit. On the Com, in their minds, they both give a teleportation order and instantly dematerialize, beaming back to the Betelgeuse.

Two hours later, Raiden, Zeina, Maia, Kurzon, and Royce meet on the Valkyrie with a minimum-sized crew to take them to Planet Artep. Raiden had an hour to spend with Oren at lunch, but it was time for Raiden to head to Artep and for his son, Oren, to head back to Karnox.

"My son, I am so very proud of the incredible man that you have become. When I finish on Artep, we will find a way to spend more time together," says Raiden as he says his farewell to Oren.

"Father, you gave me just the right combination of adversity and unconditional support. Your greatest lessons have been your examples, but I can take it from here. See you after you're done on Artep," says Oren.

Raiden beams over and joins the others on the bridge of the Valkyrie. The Valkyrie has only one center chair which Raiden gives to Zeina.

"She's your ship Zeina. Let's see what she got," says Raiden. Zeina is moving her hand on the side console. Suddenly, the sloping ceiling spanning the bridge from front to back turns translucent revealing the inside of the space dock beyond the ship. Floating below the transparent canopy is a 3D hologram of the route being charted between the Ninth Plexus in Aldebaran, and Planet Artep in Bellatrix.

"Maia, please take her out of space dock. One quarter impulse power," says Zeina. "Aye, Captain," says Maia.

The Valkyrie emerges out of its space dock with the Plexus glowing in the rearview surrounded by its complex artificial lattice structure. Thousands of starships are coming and going. Inside the ship, the 3D holographic display of the route from the Plexus to Planet Artep is adjusting its image in real-time as the ship is moving through space.

The system of cosmic ley lines guiding the traffic flow through the plexus highway interchange takes hold of the Valkyrie. Suddenly, a bright tunnel of light opens up formed by the ley lines. The ship is pulled inside the tunnel as its velocity is pushed by a force beyond the ship.

After only a few minutes, the ship is already slowing. The Valkyrie emerges from the plexus tunnel system to arrive in front of a perimeter exit gate leading to the outside of the stellar defense grid enveloping the entire Aldebaran system. Maia receives the all-clear to exit the gate.

"We're exiting the Aldebaran system now," says Maia as she pushes the throttle on her side console to pass through the stargate.

An electrical vibration is felt running through the ship when in the same moment everything outside begins rushing past the craft.

They're now beyond the defense grid moving in interstellar space. "Maia, warp six to Artep," says Ziena. "Aye, Captain. Engaging warp drive now," says Maia as she throttles forward. In a swirling green flash of light, the Valkyrie instantly achieves warp six with zero ramp-up.

Maia looks back and forth between Raiden, Zeina, and Royce and the viewscreen as something very strange just occurred.

Raiden looks over at Royce with a curious look on his face.

Royce responds to Raiden's and Maia's expressions and explains,

"Everyone, you just experienced *Trans Warp Acceleration*. We now have the technology to do it with smaller size vessels such as the Valkyrie. It involves an integration between our warp drive technology and our latest teleportation technology. Rather than moving the ship directly into warp, we teleport into warp. We can also drop out of warp in the same manner. It erases the warp signature," says Royce.

"That's Incredible! This changes the whole theater of war," says Raiden with his hand on his chin.

"I have a feeling the Valkyrie and I are going get along famously," says Zeina as she looks straight ahead with a grin on her face.

"Royce, it is my understanding that a ship can only be teleported from another source beyond the ship being teleported, and it can only be done with small-sized ships over short distances. Please explain."

"The rule still holds, Raiden. We have not overcome the rule. We are not carrying out a full point-to point-teleportation sequence. Our engineers discovered a loophole. We found that a ship could initialize its own teleportation sequence. It's only limited in completing the sequence. With this new understanding, we figured out a way to teleport into warp without having to complete the teleportation sequence. We exit the sequence through warp, not through teleportation. We can also reverse it. As long as warp is in the middle of the sequence, we can both enter and exit the sequence," explains Royce.

"Zeina, if you ever get lost in space, I'll know where you are. You will be lost somewhere in the warp zone," says Kurzon.

"Warp and teleport are just two different methods of merging with the zero-point quantum field, Kurzon. The key is knowing how to communicate with the field dynamically," explains Royce.

"Sorry, Royce, I don't speak Quantum. I can perform however, a quadriplegic bio-cephalic neural transfusion on 18 different types of humanoid brain." says Kurzon.

"That's impressive, Kurzon. But I find your Lyran Souffle even more impressive," remarks Raiden jokingly.

"All, we're arriving at Bellatrix," announces Maia as she types on her side console. They're approaching the Bellatrix stellar defense grid.

There's a bright flash of light and then suddenly they drop out of warp coasting through space with no rubber-banding effect a ship typically experiences when jumping out of warp.

"Amazing, Zeina, you will be able to sneak right up on someone," remarks Raiden.

"Not to mention we now have cloaking ability," says Royce. "Can we hide from our own ships?" asks Zeina.

Zeina looks over at Raiden. Raiden knows what she's thinking. He gives her a nod to proceed with one eyebrow raised.

"Engaging cloaking device...now," says Zeina as she slides her finger on her side console. The ship disappears from view.

"We're invisible to all other ships," says Maia as she watches her computer monitor.

"Well, let's see how invisible we actually are," says Zeina as she moves the Valkyrie out of the line of ships waiting to enter into the Bellatrix system. They're now crossing over top the other ships.

"Ah, the *Tau Orionis* is up ahead. Let's pay *Captain Theroux* a visit, shall we Raiden?" asks Zeina.

"Proceed, Zeina. M, please record this," says Raiden with a smile.

The Valkyrie drops in on the Tau Orionis, only 50 feet above her bridge completely invisible to all ship sensors on the Tau Orionis.

Raiden hits the intercom on his side console and says, "Captain Theroux of the Tau Orionis...

...are you going somewhere?"

Captain Darrian Theroux, a middle-aged man, also newly promoted to the rank of captain, is sitting in his chair confused and taken aback by Raiden's impromptu hello and comment.

"Your Majesty, what a nice surprise. We're stationed outside the Bellatrix defense perimeter. Several of our smaller ships are disembarking to various planets in the interior. We just completed our mission in Helion Prime," says Captain Theroux.

"M, override Captain Theroux's command and allow us to view the Tau Orionis bridge," says Raiden.

Suddenly the solid black angular Tau Orionis, nearly the size of the Betelgeuse, turns its bridge viewscreen fully transparent to all outside observers. Everyone on the bridge of the Valkyrie can see everyone on the bridge of the Tau Orionis, but the Tau Orionis sees only outer space.

The crew on the bridge of the Tau Orionis appears confused as they look up at the viewscreen wondering who changed the screen mode.

Raiden continues speaking to Captain Theroux,

"Ah! I see, Captain. Enjoy your shore leave. You all did a great job in Helion Prime. By the way, Captain…I like your leather jacket. Where are you going on vacation?"

Captain Theroux touches his jacket, confused. Looking around he says, "Thank you, Raiden. I'm going home to Olympia…

… but where are you, Sir?"

Raiden drops the cloak.

The Valkyrie appears hovering right over the Tau Orionis bridge. It looks like a giant black raven in space watching menacingly. The crew aboard the bridge of the Tau Orionis are stunned.

"M, allow the Tau Orionis to see who is on the bridge of the Valkyrie," says Raiden.

The Valkyrie front fuselage turns transparent.

"All, wave to our friends on the Tau Orionis," says Raiden.

Raiden, Zeina, Maia, and Kurzon are all waving with smiles. Royce watches with a perplexed expression.

Everyone begins laughing on both ships.

"Captain Theroux," meet the new Valkyrie. We're just testing her new cloaking device. She is the first Orion ship with the capability," says Raiden.

Captain Theroux is relieved and all smiles. He says,

"Magnificent, we will all be extra careful from now on. We'll never know if you're just around the corner watching us, Raiden."

Captain Theroux changes his attention toward Zeina and says, "Zeina, congratulations on your promotion. The Tau Orionis and her crew look forward to working with you and the Betelgeuse."

"Thank you, Captain. Enjoy your shore leave home on Olympia. Talk again soon," says Zeina as she waves goodbye.

CHAPTER SIX

PLANET SERAPAS

General Urlex is staring out the windows of the Scorpion flagship, the Antares, as the Orion fleet disappears among flashes of light like a lightning storm in space. The Betelgeuse and the Orion Ninth Fleet are entering warp on their way to the Aldebaran system. Commander Garrett Cartrite, standing ten feet away behind a console, is also watching the Orion fleet make its exit when he touches a communication device on his shirt and says,

"Commander Carla Benitz of the Alniyat, dispatch three teams to commandeer each of the three Orion cargo ships to secure the Xerion.

"Meet General Urlex and me at the following coordinates on Cargo Ship One in ten minutes," says Garrett as he types in the coordinates.

"Aye, Sir," says Carla Benitz from Alniyat.

A few minutes later, before leaving for Cargo Ship One, General Urlex walks up to Garrett and says in a calm, matter-of-fact voice,

"Garrett, I will not be joining you and Commander Benitz on the cargo ship. I already know we don't have the Xerion. I know what happened. I will explain it to everyone. This evening, please have all senior officers involved in the M-Trex 3 operation come to my home on Serapas for dinner at 19:00 hours. It's time for a sit-down," says the General as he stands assuredly with one hand on Garrett's console.

With a look of disbelief, Garrett says, "General, how can you possibly know already that we don't have the Xerion?"

"I have sources that no one else has, Garrett. I have eyes and ears everywhere," says the General. "Well, if that's true about the Xerion, then I take full responsibility. I failed you, Sir," says Garrett.

"Garrett, it's not your fault at all. And just between you and me, I never cared about the Xerion or M-Trex 3. We have plenty of our own Xerion already. What I care about is stoking fear in the Orion Empire and making a strong stand against them to rally our new Scorpion fleet. After the Orion are consumed enough by their own fear, it will throw them off balance. Then, they will make a big mistake. And when they do, I will be there to exploit that mistake and strike a devasting blow at the heart of the Empire. The more they fight us, the more we will consume them, and before anyone realizes it, they will all be Omicron."

"You're brilliant, Cyrus. You have my total trust. I understand your method. However, I cannot help but be deeply troubled by the M-Trex 3 mission. Something went terribly wrong," says Garrett.

"Don't think about it, Garrett. Just gather and pull our forces from M-Trex 3. We accomplished what I set out to do here. There's Orion blood in the water. The sharks smell the blood, and they're circling. Our fleet just saw us destroy a massive Orion Destroyer in only two blasts. Our Scorpion forces are rallied and energized. The Orion forces are frightened and unsure," says the General.

"Understood. But why do you want to abandon M-Trex 3? We have a forcefield lock on the whole system. We can just take it," questions Garrett.

"No, I have no interest in it. It's a distraction from our overall objective. It would draw too many of our forces to hold it and control it. We need to stay focused on the end game. All is going exactly per plan. We need to stay the course," says the General.

"I stand corrected, Sir. We will see you this evening," says Garrett.

General Urlex dematerializes from the bridge of the Antares to board his personal command ship inside the docking bay of the Antares.

His ship leaves the Antares and is heading to the Scorpion headquarter home-world, Serapas, in the Kronos star system located in the M4 Globular Cluster within the constellation of Scorpius.

The personal command ship of General Cyrus Urlex, *the Girtab*, is a glowing neon blue horseshoe shaped-craft with the two prongs of the horseshoe pointed forward like the snapping claws of a scorpion. The Girtab jumps out of warp. Planet Serapas is straight ahead.

** Let's now take a step back in time. **

Three weeks earlier, on Serapas, Senior Scorpion Officer and Omicron member, Alexander Wolf, is in a senior officer meeting at the military headquarters. Although Omicron officers, who together form a fifth column of the Scorpion Republic, had successfully foiled a plot to overthrow General Cyrus Urlex (Episode One), the Omicron Order was still maintained as a highly secretive clandestine organization.

Everyone in this meeting is a senior Omicron officer, and they all know it, but still, based on Omicron rules, no one speaks of it. To speak of it is punishable by death. The rule is always followed while on duty, especially while on deployment, or in Scorpion government or military facilities. However, when off duty, and when alone with another trusted Omicron officer, quiet conversations do take place. All official Omicron discussions between members of the Order typically only take place in the Omicron virtual reality construct known as *the Grid.*

Alex is in a classroom with about ten other officers taking notes while listening to the instructor standing at the front of the room.

Alex notices a female officer in the class who he's had a crush on ever since he first saw her and listened to her talking about work. He's never spoken to her in an unofficial manner. Alex has only seen her twice on the Grid, and in just a few other trainings in the real world. This time around, he can't help himself. He keeps looking across the room at her. She notices and returns one of his glances with a smile.

That smile of hers was just enough to send his heart racing. He feels like a kid again. After class is finished, she decides to lean against the wall near the classroom door to look at an old book, hoping that he will stop and say hello as he leaves the class.

They don't know each other's names yet. It's Scorpion protocol never to blurt out names and ranks in a group. They never do roll calls. However, it's perfectly fine to introduce yourself privately and share your name and rank. Just don't ever say you are Omicron.

There's something exotic and mysterious about her, but it's hard to say exactly what it is. It must be the whole combination of personality, intelligence, voice, mannerisms, appearance, maybe even pheromones. Alex takes the opportunity and walks up to her and says,

"Wow, I used to have an old book just like that."

"Really?" she questions with a smile as she closes the book and glances up at him with an ominous look in her eyes.

She continues talking. "What was the name of your book?" Her hand is covering the book's title.

Alex stops to think with a grin on his face.

"Ah, yes! I remember now. It was called

"Doctor Ned's Field Guide to Bird Watching.

"It was an old book that my mother had given me," says Alex.

She responds,

"So, you like watching birds?"

"It's not something I would set out to do by itself. I like hiking. While hiking, I like knowing what it is that I'm looking at when I see the various birds, animals, plants, and trees," explains Alex.

She interjects wittingly,

"Wait a second; you're not the cute, smart, dorky type, are you?"

Alex answers quickly in an equal manner,

"Umm…. they do say I'm like a human encyclopedia."

"Oh, gee. That's going to be a problem," she comments while looking down shaking her head. She looks back up at him with one eyebrow raised and a smirk.

"Why's that a problem?" asks Alex.

"Because that's my favorite type," she answers as she gathers her bag and starts heading for the door.

"Wait, I don't even know your name," says Alex

She answers,

"My name is Erin. I am Senior Officer Erin Devereux."

He reaches out to shake her hand and replies,

"Nice to meet you, Erin. My name is Alex. I am Senior Officer Alexander Wolf."

Erin shakes his hand and says, "It's nice to meet you too, Alex, but I have somewhere else I must go."

She turns and starts walking to the door.

"Wait, when can we see each other again?" asks Alex as he speaks to her back. Erin stops, turns around, and says,

"Tomorrow night, Café LaRoche, 21:00 hours. It's the only chance you will ever get, Alex. So, don't miss it."

She turns back around and walks out the door.

It's the next evening. Alex is walking across a green field at night on the campus of the Scorpion military headquarters. It's part of the underground city of Og, the capital city of Serapas, where Alex lives.

Like the Orion, the engineers of the Scorpius Republic know how to make light pass from beyond a planet's atmosphere into the interior of its deep subterranean city-states. *Circe*, the only moon orbiting Planet Serapas, is illuminating the night sky. Nearby, a group of men and women are playing a soccer game under a group of tall field lights.

Alex is headed toward a rectangular opening among a group of trees. He stops before the opening. It's showing nothing but a continuation of the same trees beyond. A computerized voice speaks from the opening and says,

"State your destination."

Alex responds and says,

"City of Tet, Waterfront and Fifth."

The voice speaks again and says,

"Proceed across the threshold."

Alex walks across the threshold and suddenly the whole environment changes. He's on the waterfront in the underground city of Tet on the other side of the planet. It looks a lot like the neighborhood of Georgetown in Washington, DC - millions of years in the future on Earth.

On Serapas, they mix old styles with modern technology while making the modern technology disappear from sight. To see the technology is considered crude and ugly.

The old city of Tet has stately brick architecture similar to the way Georgetown would later become. It has cobblestone roads with shops and restaurants lining the streets. However, the shops and restaurants are owned and run by single proprietors, literally, mom-and-pop shops that have been there for generations as family-run businesses.

Tet doesn't have cars on its streets. The streets are only for people. On Serapas, people only use teleportals like the one Alex just walked through. The teleportals are strictly controlled, however. They don't take anyone off-world or to the surface of Serapas.

Alex and Erin met up, ate dinner, and chit-chatted over small stuff for a couple of hours while getting to know each other. After dinner, Erin says, "So, Alex, are you ready for dessert? They have a killer key lime pie here," as she picks up a glass to sip a frothy dark malted beer.

"Absolutely, key lime pie is one of my favorites," says Alex.
The waiter comes to their table, takes their orders, and then walks away.
Erin has something on her mind. She's staring at the foam of her beer
while twisting her cup with her hand and looks up and says,

"So, Alex, how much do you actually know about the Order?"
Alex is just gazing back at her speechless for a minute, thinking about
how to respond. They both know they shouldn't be talking about it and
are careful not to say the word Omicron. If it were anyone else, Alex
would just get up and walk away.

"I think you and I probably know all the same things, Erin.
We've both been to the same places. You know what I'm talking
about," says Alex.

"Yes, Alex, but do you realize that there are two sides to the Order?
Both sides agree on the same overall goal. But each side has a different
culture, so to speak. Both have…different perspectives if you will,"
says Erin.

"I'm not familiar with this level of nuance, Erin. Is it really that
important? After all, everyone agrees on the same principal objective.
We all support our leader, right?" argues Alex.

"Yes, of course, Alex. But it's much more than just nuance.
The rabbit hole runs much deeper. There are doors beyond doors."

Erin now has Alex's interest. He's curious about what she knows.
"You have my interest, Erin. Take me down the rabbit hole,"
says Alex.

Erin takes out a pen, writes a word on a napkin, folds the napkin,
and then passes it across the table to Alex.

Alex opens the napkin to read the word. It says, *Gorgon.*
He closes the napkin and just stares back at Erin without saying a word.

Erin says, "Do you know what that is, Alex?"
Alex says, "Yes, I know what it is. I've actually seen her once."

"Do you know what her role and function is?" asks Erin.
"It was explained briefly to me once, but I doubt I know everything or
that I fully understand it," responds Alex.

"That's an honest answer," says Erin.
Erin takes the napkin from Alex, tears the word off, and places it over
the candle flame on the table. It burns and turns to smoke and ashes.
Erin writes another name, folds the napkin, and passes it to Alex.

Alex takes the napkin from Erin and opens it. It says, *Altimus.*

Alex looks at it, thinks about it, and then looks back up with one eyebrow raised.

"Do you know what that is, Alex?"

Alex says, "No...I can't say I know what it is."

"Many don't know, Alex. Even many of the mansion goers, don't know. But to know, you have to be a mansion goer," says Erin. *(She's referring to the Omicron mansion located on the Grid, the VR Program)*

"What does it mean, Erin? This word, what does it mean?" questions Alex as he touches the napkin with the word, *Altimus.*"

"The goal of the Order is to bring about a unity of humanities, to direct us all to a higher order of existence, to maximize our ultimate potential. But the question is, what do we do once we get there? Have you ever thought about that, Alex?"

"Gee...I don't know, live life peacefully. See what comes next. Why does it matter, Erin?" questions Alex?

"It matters. Because if we don't have a purpose after we reach our goal of unification, we'll get lost again and lose everything we fought to gain. We always need a purpose.

"The second question that arises is: Does every purpose need a problem to solve or an adversary to fight?

"Because if that's true, we will unconsciously seek to find the adversary from within and create a problem to solve. That problem will break us apart once again until it turns into a vicious cycle," explains Erin.

"So then...what's the solution, Erin?" inquires Alex as he takes a piece of his pie with his fork.

"That brings us to the two sides of the Order, Alex. On the one hand, we have *G*. On the other hand, we have *A*. Both have opposing views on what comes next," explains Erin.

Alex chimes in with his opinion,

"From what I know, I would say *G* is all about controlling and managing people's perception to maintain unity. It utilizes authority, organization, and force to maintain power. I'm not sure there is any other way, Erin. The law of entropy dictates that all things trend toward chaos and decay. It takes will, authority, and control to keep it all together. I hate to say it, but the purpose of what comes next is obviously the maintenance of that power and control."

Erin rebuts, "That's the police-state solution. It exemplifies well the *G* side of the Order. But, Alex, there is another much more sustainable solution offered by the *A* side. Do you wish to know what that is?"

"Of course, I have an open mind, Erin. I'm not set on any one solution," says Alex. Erin takes the other piece of the napkin and places it over the candle fire. As the flame is flickering between them, Erin says, "Then tomorrow night, I will show you the other side. It is much better to be shown than be told. It is the only way to truly understand."

Erin and Alex split the tab and make their way out of the restaurant. They start walking down the street toward the waterfront.

"Alex, normally after dinner, I would say let's go for a walk or go see a show, but I think its best that we say goodbye now and pick this up right here tomorrow night," says Erin. Alex stops walking and says,

"Okay, sounds like a plan. That was a great conversation at dinner, and I absolutely loved the food. Thank you for taking me there. Should we meet right here tomorrow night?"

"You're welcome, Alex! It's so refreshing to talk to someone in the real world about this stuff. I can't wait for tomorrow. And, yes, let's meet right here at 22:00 hours. Agreed?"

"Agreed, that's perfect." Alex gently touches Erin's hand goodbye and begins walking toward the waterfront while looking back and says,

"See you tomorrow." Erin, while walking away, looks back at Alex and waves with a smile. She continues walking 20 feet in the opposite direction from Alex, passes into a teleportal, and disappears.

The next day Alex can't wait to see Erin again. After their first date, he's more enthralled with her than ever. Alex can't stop thinking about her. Every time he looks up at the clock, it's like it's not even moving, and he gets a rush of butterflies in his stomach. In his mind, the combination of Erin's beauty and intellect is intoxicating. Even the memory of her perfume keeps creeping back into his thoughts.

Then there's the whole mystery about Erin talking about the two sides of the Omicron. One side is the Gorgon. It represents fear-based control and the manipulation of perception (delusion). He remembers Garrett saying the Gorgon was the Omicron Oracle and an aberration of the virtual construct. The Gorgon arises out of the naturally occurring neurosynaptic grid underlying the fabric of space. Then there is the Altimus side of the Omicron. What can that be? Alex has no idea.

Finally, the much-anticipated hour has arrived. Alex is already back at their meeting point. He's waiting only a couple of minutes under a streetlight when Erin comes walking out of the same teleportal she had disappeared into the night before. They're both all smiles as they greet each other. Erin touches Alex's arm and points with her other hand to a direction down a side street and says, "Shall we?"

They're walking down a block of gated brick homes lining the streets. They have a stately architecture. Big old trees and manicured hedges surround the homes. Erin is leading the way as the couple turn down a smaller side street leading to a steep set of old stone steps.

They descend the steps and walk a short distance to an old home sunk inland toward the back. Its lights are off. It almost looks abandoned. Erin walks up the side walkway of the house and enters its backyard. Alex looks up and sees all the stars shining brightly in the sky. The scent of a freshly cut lawn permeates the air. Erin stands at his side and looks up with a smile. A shooting star crisscrosses the firmament.

"Alex, look at me," says Erin as she takes his hand. Alex turns around with a gentle smile on his face to see what Erin has to say.

"I like you, Alex. So, I have to be honest with you. There is only one way we can be together, and it's through the door I am about to take you. But I have to warn you; once I take you through, there is no turning back. Once you know Altimus, you will always know it, and it will always know you. Your knowledge of it will become a burden to you because it will be another dimension of the darkness most of the world is just not ready to learn about. I wish I could tell you what it is before showing it to you, but I cannot. It's forbidden. I'm taking a risk letting you know that I even know about it," says Erin.

Alex feels apprehensive following her, considering everything she has shared, but his desire for her is getting the best of him. He's also curious to learn about what Erin claims is the other side of the Omicron.

"If you want to know, Alex, then follow me," says Erin.

Erin begins walking away further into the darkness of the backyard before almost disappearing from view.

Alex is standing still watching Erin walk away into the darkness. He shakes his head for a second and says to himself, "Damn, alright! This is crazy!" And then he follows after her.

Alex catches up with Erin, who smiles at his arrival. At the corner of the backyard, there's a big tree. Next to the tree is a small yard shed with an old rusty door. Erin opens the door. They step inside.

Erin closes the door behind them. It's pitch-black. Alex can't see his hand in front of his face. A crack of light bursts through the other side as Erin opens another door about eight feet in front of them. There's a staircase beyond the second door leading down into a basement. The stairs are made of smooth slabs of stone with a vaulted ceiling of rustic stones lined with a few yellow lights spaced apart to illuminate the steps leading down.

"This looks ominous," remarks Alex.
"No worries, Alex. I will protect you," says Erin jokingly as she leads the way down the stairs.

They're both laughing.
They get to the bottom of the stairs and turn the corner. What started as a garden shed that then turned into a wine-cellar-like stairway leading into a dark basement, has turned into a stunning baroque style parlor room made of fine hardwoods, marble, and exquisite furniture.

Erin takes Alex's hand, walks to the center of the room, turns, and starts kissing him. Alex responds passionately with the unleashing of his pent-up fires of Eros.

Clothes are flying as they both lose themselves inside the rapture of their first embrace. Erin takes Alex's hand once more and leads him into another room. It's a bed chamber with a bed covered in white satin.

As Alex and Erin are in the throes of bliss, naked and bare, blankets moving like the sea, hands grasping, toes curling, kisses aflame, the bed starts moving down into a large room below. Alex doesn't even notice that's he's now in a different room as Erin's whole body moves upon him while entwined in full erotic embrace.

Two other women are now slowly crawling up on the bed alongside Erin, running their hands along Alex's muscular body.

Startled to realize he has company, Alex looks into Erin's eyes with an expression of surprise. She returns his look with radiant reassuring eyes to let him know everything is okay and intentional.

Alex looks on either side of him to see the large room he is in. Shockingly, it's full of naked men and women in a rampage of sexual indulgence in a multitude of various forms and combinations.

The erotic storm of Eros has subsided. Alex and Erin are now sitting at a small round marble table with fancy chairs, sipping tiny glasses of Port wine. Across the room, the merrymaking continues.

At the perimeter of the room, other couples are seated at small tables and couches being served by scantily clad waiters and waitresses. Vibrant music with deep bass tones fills the dimly lit room adorned with masterfully created erotic artwork and statues.

"This, Alex, is Altimus," says Erin, pointing to the party."

"Wow! All I can say is wow!" says Alex.

"There's a purpose behind it all, Alex," replies Erin.

"My mind is open. I am all ears, Erin. Please explain how this is the other side of Omicron. How is this part of the solution to what comes after the Omicron achieves unity throughout the galaxy?"

Erin explains,

"Altimus is *Desire*. The Gorgon is *Control.*

"The two form the Axis of the Omicron behavioral complex as part of its genetic program. The Omicron recognizes and utilizes the most primitive basic functions of human nature rather than fighting them. We embrace them and direct them to a higher harmony."

"I agree with that, Erin. That's a fundamental tenet of our Order," says Alex as he adjusts to listen more closely to what Erin is saying.

Erin continues,

"In the mind, it may look like control is in charge, as it's often the one calling the shots. However, what drives the need for control?"

Alex answers, "Desire?"

"Not directly, but you're close. The primary driver in the human mind's need for control is *Fear*. This is why all our commanders are trained to utilize fear as a mechanism for controlling the ranks and manipulating our enemies. But what comes before fear?" asks Erin.

Alex chimes in, "That's where desire must come in. We fear to lose what we desire," says Alex.

"That's right, Alex. And what comes before desire is *Perception.* We desire or covet what we perceive we need to survive and reproduce. When that desire is compromised in some way, fear arises in the mind. Following fear is the instinct to control what we perceive the threat to be. This is how we assuage our fear. If we can't achieve control to assuage the fear, the next defense the mind builds is *Delusion.* The mind creates a fake reality and persona to escape the pain of its own fear," says Erin.

Alex responds,

"Ultimately, what we truly desire and strive for is more *Life.* Pleasure is what we feel when we gain a deeper sensation of life. Therefore, what we ultimately fear is *Death* and *Pain,* the opposites of *Life* and *Pleasure.* The Omicron are trained to utilize fear, death, and pain to control people. People are easily controlled through fear because of their desires."

"Exactly right again, Alex. The utilization of fear and control to achieve the Omicron aims has been proven to work, but is this honestly how we want to live our lives indefinitely after achieving our aims? It's unsustainable. Fear-based control is prone to spontaneous self-destruction. Rebellions always ensue. Everything achieved breaks apart, and we end up in a vicious cycle of trying to regain control," says Erin.

"And the Altimus solution is what exactly?" asks Alex.
Erin explains,

"The Altimus approach is based on the premise that after the Omicron achieves power and control throughout the galaxy, the only possible purpose left is humanity's continuous exploration of itself. If we take the shackles off that purpose, we honestly believe this will be sufficient to maintain peace, stability, and unity without end. Anything short of that will fail."

Alex chimes in,

"And how do you prevent that approach from breaking down, Erin? If you keep feeding the first beast (desire), the second beast (control), eventually follows, and when it does, it rises even bigger," says Alex.

Erin continues explaining,

"Great point, Alex. Indeed, it has broken down in many past experimental attempts. But we now have a stable working formula. It's been working now for a long time. In all past failed attempts, people were always left to their own devices in how they explored their various human relationships and how they set boundaries. The problem is, as mere individual mortals, when alone, we sense our vulnerability and limitations to fulfill our own most basic needs and, voila, fear seeps into our minds and the second beast arises."

Alex interrupts, "Exactly, Erin. For example, people fearing that they may lose their desired partners to other people. They're constantly drawn to control that which they desire, in this case, their partners.

"You got it, Alex. That's where it always breaks down. You can't just give someone something they desire if what comes along with it is the fear of losing it, and therefore the need to control it," says Erin.

"So, what's the solution? How do we give people the freedom of human exploration without the associated fear of loss and the need to control the perceived threat of that loss?" asks Alex. Erin answers,

"The key, Alex, is not fostering and enabling an entitled feeling of control over anyone. We do this by bringing people into a collective where they are never left to meet their needs on their own, but where they constantly sense and trust the support of others in the collective. We have a few basic rules in Altimus to promote this.

"No partnering. Everyone lives alone. We all belong to each other. Ironically, living alone is part of the solution. But we are all nearby and available to each other. Jealousy and the need to possess another person are not tolerated and are grounds for immediate expulsion from Altimus.

"There are many other benefits to this approach, including one's internal development, and the more time and energy it allows people to devote to their vocations. We believe in constantly experiencing new and different relationships. It's not only sexual. These relationships exist on every human level, absent fear and control. Consequently, each relationship is more beneficial in an individual's personal development. It opens up multiple human dimensions of purpose, experience, and fulfillment. We've found through case studies that this provides enough purpose and stimulation in life that people won't seek to overturn the system, but will instead vigorously seek to maintain it.

"This lifestyle is facilitated only between members of Altimus who understand and respect the rules. Once you are expelled, you're never allowed back in. Our devotion to each other is paramount. We're family. If any of our members are ever in trouble, we all arrive to support them. It is critical that no one in our Order ever feels they are being left to their own devices. You cannot serve the Gorgon and Altimus at the same time. If you ever submit to fear, delusion, and control, you will be expelled. We periodically run brain scans to know if you are sustaining the correct state of mind to remain in the Order. You cannot fool it. "

"And what about love?" asks Alex. Erin responds,

"People get confused about love, Alex. Love doesn't seek exclusivity and control. We believe that we love better by loving many people, not just one. Every person shows us a different face of God. Why limit ourselves to knowing only one or just a few faces of God?" We should seek to know God in all the infinite forms of its expression. This is what makes life worth living. This is what gives us purpose."

"Agreed, Erin," says Alex as he adjusts his body in his chair with his finger on his head thinking about everything. Alex continues,

"So, how does this all reconcile with the Omicron?" he asks.

"We support the overall objective of the Omicron, and we follow all Omicron rules, including Omicron secrecy. To be a member of Altimus, you must already be a member of the Omicron Order in good standing. And you must already be on the Grid. If you reveal your membership in Altimus to anyone, then you're exposing your Omicron membership, and that, unfortunately, is punishable by death.

"That's it, Alex. That's our code. And that's why I had to bring you here if you wanted to know me any further. You're part of Altimus now. If you wish to reject that membership now, that's fine. But you will never be allowed back again, and you and I will not be together again."

Alex takes a moment and then raises his glass and says, "Hail Omicron-Altimus!" Erin smiles and raises her glass.

** We are now back in the present day. **

General Urlex is arriving home after having left the Antares via his command ship, the Girtab. He's walking up a front walkway to a large, beautiful, three-story Victorian-style-looking home in the outskirts of the underground city of Og surrounded by a forest on Planet Serapas. This is one of the few places on Serapas requiring a land vehicle to arrive. Teleporting into or near the General's home is strictly forbidden, as with other leaders of the Order. A long winding road leads to his estate. As you would expect, his house is large with a team of servants, cooks, and security personnel. Cooking is one of General Urlex's specialties. He loves to entertain to show off his numerous abilities.

Usually, the Omicron Order would only ever meet on the Grid, but the General has something special planned for him and the senior Omicron officers invited to his home this evening. As the head of the Order, the General has the authority to make such an exception.

The General is in his chef's kitchen with an apron on cooking at the big stove. The kitchen is abuzz with activity. General Urlex has 30 senior Omicron officers coming to his home in just a few hours. These particular officers were all involved in the M-Trex conflict with the Orion. The dining room is being set up. Classical music is playing. Servers are walking the home getting ready for the guests to arrive.

The guests begin arriving. They're pulling up inside autonomous self-driving vehicles to a circular stone-paved area in front of the home. Fire lamps line a driveway of crushed stone leading up to the house. A beautifully manicured lawn separates the mansion from the forest beyond, giving one haunting chills when looking at the wooded realm from afar. Everyone is arriving alone. No partners or guests are allowed at this gathering as official Omicron business will be discussed.

Most of the senior Omicron officers have arrived, including Commander Garrett Cartrite and the senior officers of the Antares, along with Alex Wolf and Carla Benitz of the Alniyat, among others. Some lower-ranked senior officers of different ships are seeing each for the first time in the real world off the Grid. On the Grid, they already know each other.

Alex is also noticing a few familiar faces he happens to know are members of Altimus, and they're also noticing Alex, but of course, they're quiet about it. Members of the Omicron Order don't know the members of Omicron-Altimus unless they themselves are Altimus. Altimus is a sanctum within sanctums, but it's not a power structure; it's just a culture and a way of life for a segment of the Omicron.

Neither Garrett Cartrite nor General Urlex is a member of Altimus. Garrett and the General are devout faithful followers of the Gorgon. You're either a follower of the Gorgon, or you're a follower of Altimus. You cannot be both. They have diametrically opposing views but share the same ultimate Omicron goal. The General is quite aware of Altimus, but that's another whole story. Garrett really has no idea about Altimus, and he would never be approached to join. He's too far gone down the Gorgon rabbit hole. On a personal level, someone who fits the Altimus profile, and someone who fits the Gorgon profile, hate each other with a passion. On a technical level, they're capable of working together to achieve a higher goal they both agree with, as long as they don't get too personal with one another. Otherwise, it all falls apart.

After an hour of socializing, hors d'oeuvres, and cocktails, everyone is being called to the large dining room. The General surely knows how to put the charm on when he needs to. He loves being the center of attention and reciprocates in turn with entertaining his guests. As everyone is sitting down in their chairs, the General is standing at the head of the table, tapping his glass with a fork to get everyone's attention. He begins speaking,

"Everyone, everyone, please quiet down. Thank you for coming to my Serapas estate this evening. This is the first time for many of you. For dinner, I went all-out and personally prepared the three main dishes of the seven-course tasting menu that you are all about to eat and enjoy. I tasted them already. Trust me; they're superb. I also brought in the greatest musicians on Serapas to entertain us during dinner. And, of course, we're opening bottles of the finest wines in the galaxy."

Everyone is clapping. The General continues,

"I wanted to host a dinner for you all this evening to thank each of you for your tremendous work at M-Trex 3. The Orion came in confident and left with their tails between their legs, very unsure of themselves. For the first time ever, an Orion destroyer was destroyed, and not just destroyed, but blown to smithereens in only two shots from the Antares. Trust me, they're terrified now. We also took M-Trex 3 and its moons hostage inside our own forcefields put in place by our core of engineers. A spectacular job with months of preparation! The man in charge of the core of engineers is Captain Ty Kalek. Captain, please stand for everyone."

Everyone applauds the captain as he stands and takes a bow.

"Captain Kalek, I always reward excellence, loyalty, and hard work! You are hereby promoted to Scorpion Commander. I've also instructed our treasury to transfer one ton of Xerion to your personal bank vault. You are now a very, very wealthy man.

"All take note. This can be you. I have already made other officers wealthy and I will continue to do so when you exceed my expectations and demonstrate unflinching loyalty to me and our cause.

"Let's enjoy our meal now, and then after dinner, I have prepared a special demonstration for you all," says the General.

While everyone is eating, the officers are charged up and talking. Garrett is telling stories about how the General had rewarded him and other officers following other successful campaigns.

Alex is listening intently to it all. The Altimus members have eyes on each other but don't go any further than that. The General is busy at the end of the table talking about his recipes, how he masterfully prepared the food, and his extensive culinary training.

During the second to last course, the General gets up, joins the musicians, and starts playing an alto saxophone to the tune of jazz music. He's bouncing around the other musicians having a great time. Several of the Omicron officers are clapping and dancing. After his third song, the food has finally finished. Everyone is sipping on after-dinner drinks. The General comes to the front of the room and says,

"Everyone, can I please have your attention one more time. Thank you! I hope you all enjoyed the meal and the music!

"Although we had a largely successful engagement with the Orion, there is just one loose end. We never did capture the Xerion. Now don't get me wrong, I honestly don't care about Xerion at all. It was more of a powerplay than anything. We already have massive treasuries of Xerion. A large portion of all known Xerion mining planets in the galaxy belongs to Scorpius. M-Trex 3 belongs to the Orion. Let them have it. We tested our fleet against theirs, and we kicked their ass. They ran away scared as hell. We won that battle. That's all I care about.

While the General is talking, all the servers and helpers are being quietly and quickly ushered out of the room by secret service agents. Meanwhile, the General continues speaking.

"However. The reason we didn't capture the Xerion is that we had two spies in our midst. Two of our Omicron brothers sold us out," says the General as he pushes a button on a device he's holding.

Tall flowing dark red drapes, stretching from floor to ceiling, begin pulling back to reveal a transparent glass divider wall with another room beyond the glass divider. In the room beyond, horrors of horrors, two Omicron men are completely nude and tied up lying flat on stretchers while being tortured to death by two Omicron doctors.

A pool of human blood, limbs, guts, and vomit cover the floor. The General hits another button so everyone can hear the two men crying and screaming. Alex is appalled when he realizes the two are Altimus. He and the other Altimus members are looking at each other pale white in complete shock and terror. Alex runs out of the room to puke his guts up in a garbage can. The General continues speaking casually to the group as they all squirm in their chairs in horror.

"These are spies and traitors of the Republic. I always find them. And I always will. I have eyes and ears planted everywhere at all times. I have double agents embedded among our most fierce adversaries who feed me all kinds of intelligence. Take a good look and never forget. This can be you. This can even be family members of yours.

"If you choose to give your life against the Omicron, I promise you, I will go after your whole family and torture them and kill them in the same manner as these two men. I'm sorry if this upset you, but it was necessary. It's a training exercise. Pure and simple. I bid you all a good evening. I will see you tomorrow," says the General.

Everyone is hustling out of the big room, completely terrified. Garrett is sitting back watching everyone while he casually leans against the wall with his hands folded together like it's no big deal. He's glancing at the General, his mentor, with great admiration.

All the guests have left except for Garrett. Outside the room, secret service agents guard the doors as all the land vehicles begin to pull away.

Garrett walks up to the General and says, "Sir, I can clean up here if you wish. You can just leave it to me," says Garrett.

"That's quite alright, Garrett. You go on home. I'm not done with our spies just yet. I will see you tomorrow," says the General.

"Very well, Sir," says Garrett as he takes his leave of the General. The General heads inside the torture chamber and says,

"Doctors, please leave us." One of the doctors says,

"Sorry, General, one of the men just died. He had a heart attack. We tried keeping him alive as long as possible. This one on the right is still living, however."

"Very well, please leave us," says the General as the doctors leave.

The General looks into the man's eyes, who is still barely alive. His eyes are full of pain and terror. The man says,

"General, I'm innocent. I'm not a spy. I never betrayed you." The General says, "Oh, I already know you're innocent." He pauses to gloat over him and then continues, "I used you to teach the other officers a lesson and to show everyone I am still very much in control."

Confused, the man questions, "But why me?" The General says,

"You're Altimus! And I f#@% hate Altimus! I tolerate it and use it to my strategic advantage to control weak-minded fools such as yourself. You're a bunch of disgusting, perverted degenerates. Sexual desire and eroticism exist beneath the noble virtues of human existence. It compels fear, jealousy, and chaos. I removed every ounce of it from my mind."

The dying man speaks in a slow, soft voice, saying,

"The only thing you removed is your humanity, Cyrus. You worship the Gorgon."

The General is visibly irritated by the comment and says,

"That's a bastardized pronunciation of her real name. I allow that word to persist to keep her real name a secret so others cannot summon her. But I will tell you what her real name is since you're about to die." The General leans over and whispers in his ear,

"She is the *Kiraphon.* She is the oldest living being of all creation."

The General pulls away from the man's ear and pulls out a long surgical device from a tray. The man talks back with as much strength as he can muster and says,

"You're insane, Cyrus. Your fear of losing power has made you delusional. The Gorgon is nothing but an aberration. We've only ever seen her in the virtual construct. Your Gorgon compelled delusions have given your warped mind a false cohesion of purpose and focus. Your kind always self-destructs." General Urlex responds,

"You mock what you do not know or understand. She is real. She exists beyond the Grid. She rises out of the essence of matter to bring order to chaos within the mind. She is the beginning, the end, and the one that is many. All my wealth and power came from her."

"She is the chaos! You've gone completely mad!" shouts the man.

Cyrus ignores the man and recants a prayer to the Gorgon, offering the man to her as a sacrifice. Cyrus prays to the Gorgon for power, fortune, and the ability to defeat the Orion Empire.

He then takes the man's life with the long, sharp surgical device. As he kills the man, he gets a rush of power. It gets him off sexually. He's a psychopath. His sexual pleasure is dark, twisted, and sadistic.

The General leaves the room. The doctors are standing outside. "They're all yours. Both are dead," says the General as he walks away.

CHAPTER SEVEN

THE EDGE OF BARSTOW

Twilight's sunders of angel's light and fathom's darkness reveals but an eerie narrow scapes of dreams. A place where shadows stir from corners amidst a mind's flickering flames. In this space, something rises, and the unknown becomes known. We now return to Barstow to finish the story of what happened to Lord Giao when he had reached the cathedral atop Visndorf Mountain on the dark side of the moon at the very edge of light and darkness.

Lord Giao's journey to the forbidden world of Barstow occurred six months before the events on Planet Serapas, the battle of M-Trex 3, and the historic discovery of the Permian Anomaly on Planet Artep.

While riding Areion horses, Lord Giao and the two scientists, Ann and Hector, and the two trackers, Cisco and Jada, reach a wooden drawbridge. They're waiting for a couple of minutes when a little man, only about three feet tall with a long red beard dressed in overalls and a funny sock-like brown hat, waddles out from underneath the bridge and approaches them. He walks up to Cisco with his hand out and says in a squeaky little voice, "One big coin for passage please."

Cisco has the coin ready and places it in his hand. The little troll waddles over to the bridge and lowers it. The team crosses the bridge. This is where we left off the story in the earlier chapter, and where we now pick back up. Oddly, as soon as they reach the other side of the drawbridge, the light in the air becomes dimmer and redder.

Giao notices the sudden shift in light and looks over at Hector. Hector knows Giao is reacting to the abrupt change in light and says,

"Another form of high strangeness, Your Majesty. It's something we cannot yet explain. However, we have a working hypothesis.

"We believe our higher position in hyperspace is amplifying a dynamic which exists on all worlds with life, but typically goes unseen. On Barstow and Jenesis, we can actually see it. All around us, there are valleys and plateaus in the psychic energy exchanged between the species to inform, affect, and guide the evolution of life within the biosphere. It's a system of self-regulation. It's an innate operation of the noosphere, or planetary group mind, if you will.

"We just walked into a sunken valley, or negative depression zone. Psychic energy is being drawn out of this area. Our higher position in hyperspace is allowing us to witness or see the change in the noosphere.

"Conversely, there are plateaus or positive vortex zones which shift upward in light," says Hector.

"Interesting, I wonder what is sucking the energy out of this area," says Giao. Ann chimes in,

"We believe the uneven disbursement of psychic energy into valleys and plateaus within the noosphere is following a geometric pattern impressed upon it from either a higher level of hyperspace we cannot yet detect, or from the Barstow moon's magnetosphere."

"But why would the priesthood place its cathedral inside a negative depression zone?" asks Giao. Jada answers,

"It can be for a few reasons, but the most likely one is that there are more metaphysical phenomena in a negative depression zone. The lull or depression in energy creates a destabilizing effect. It causes things to jar loose or become unglued, so to speak. The priesthood thought this dynamic made the place special and wanted to be near it."

"That makes sense, Jada," says Giao as he ponders in his mind what could possibly happen in a space that has become *unglued.*

They're approaching Visndorf mountain. The ancient cathedral on top of the summit is a sight to behold. It's made of megalithic stone construction. It's naturally built with only gravity holding it all together, but it was engineered, cut, and moved into place with a superior Orion technology from thousands of years earlier in history. Pyramid-shaped construction lends itself well to megalithic stone construction, and, indeed, the Orion had constructed many megalithic stone pyramids throughout the galaxy. However, the Visndorf cathedral was not a pyramid. The cathedral is a compilation of giant stone spires grouped together like an assembly of organ pipes.

The group stops to look at the cathedral from afar. Giao remarks, "All I can say is, the Orion have built some truly bizarre buildings over the course of time. This, however, is the strangest I've seen yet."

"It's still at least another 20 minutes up the mountain from here. The Areions will take us only to the base of the cathedral. After that, we are on our own to climb the steps," says Cisco.

They're slowly moving along a winding dirt road spiraling up the side of the mountain. A steep precipice is building alongside them. The scene is eerie. Everything is basked in a perpetual red twilight glow. It hardly changes. Occasionally, it gets as dark as night when clouds blanket the sky. However, very few clouds are in the sky on this day as the Bellatrix sun peaks above the horizon to cast its strange red glow.

As the group makes their way up the mountain, the horses are getting agitated. They keep snorting and stomping their feet. A minute later, there's a strange metallic gong sound reverberating throughout the atmosphere with an echo tailing off between intervals.

Bauwowwowwowwow, Bauwowwowwowwow, Bauwowwowwowwow.

"Your Majesty, are you aware of any military operations in the vicinity of Barstow?" asks Hector.

"It's forbidden. The only craft allowed near Erawan's two moons are those pre-approved by my father, and he's not allowing any more shuttle flights while I'm on the surface. How about the Equinox?"

"That's definitely not the Equinox," says Ann. "It sounds like a sonic technology, but we know there's no such technology on the surface," says Cisco.

The sound repeats. Everyone is carefully listening, trying to figure out from what direction it's coming. It sounds multidirectional.

"All, I hate to say it. But I don't think it's any form of technology. It's most likely a psychokinetic anomaly in response to our presence in this area of the noosphere," says Jada.

"It's a valid hypothesis, Jada," says Ann. The horses are still snorting and stomping a bit.

Giao is watching and listening to the conversation. "This place is so strange. I'm starting to understand why it's a forbidden world," says Giao.

They continue climbing the steep winding road up the mountain braving the harrowing precipice alongside them.

"It certainly seems the old priesthood wanted to discourage visitors to the cathedral," remarks Giao.

"Indeed, this was their objective, Your Majesty. With their ancient manuscripts kept on a quarantined world inside an old cathedral atop a foreboding mountain, the manuscripts are sure to last for many more generations of time," answers Ann.

They arrive at the base of the cathedral as they approach a small wooden stable for the horses. A little elf comes out to greet the team. Cisco jumps off his horse to speak with the elf.

"Hello, Sir, my name is Cisco, and these are my friends. Can you take care of our horses for two nights?" asks Cisco of the elf.

"My name is Warwick. We saw you coming up the mountain. We're happy to take care of the horses. We remember them. They've been here before. Five big coins please," says Warwick.

The others are getting off their horses watching Cisco deal with Warwick who is only about three feet tall. He has pale green-colored skin, big round blue eyes, pointy ears, small hands, and a long nose. He's wearing brown-colored overalls with a white long-sleeved shirt underneath, as well as a pair of worn black rounded shoes and a cone-shaped brown hat drooping behind his head. Cisco hands him the coins.

"Warwick, can I introduce you to my friends," asks Cisco as he points to the group."

Warwick smiles and starts walking up to the team. His first interest is with the horses which immediately show a liking to him. The whole group is talking for a couple of minutes when Giao interjects,

"Warwick, we heard a strange gong noise about 20 minutes ago when we were climbing the mountain. Do you know what that was?"

"Sir, the secret of the Barstow moon is that you and the land are one. As you thrive, the land will thrive. As you perish, the land will perish. What you heard was for you, and you alone," says Warwick as he easily climbs atop one of the horses.

Giao is just staring at Warwick, thinking, "Wow, such deep philosophical ideas and insights from an elf." Cisco steps up and says,

"Thanks, Warwick. Back in two days," as they begin to walk away.

Lord Giao and the group are walking toward the Visndorf Cathedral. Its giant stone spires are rising above the trees in the twilight's red glow. They reach the base of the cathedral and look upward at the 100 steps leading toward the doorway of the temple.

"They definitely didn't want anyone carrying anything in or out," remarks Giao.

Giao decides to take the lead climbing the steps with the others tailing close behind. At about a quarter of the way up, Giao looks toward the top of the steps and sees a man with a long all-white beard in all-white clothes sitting yoga style with his legs crossed and his back straight, waiting motionless like an old fakir. Giao turns around to Cisco, who is right behind him, and says,

"Do you see that old man at the top of the steps?"
Cisco looks up at the top of the steps and says, "No, I see nothing."

Giao turns back around, and no one is there.
A moment later, after several more steps,

Jada, right behind Cisco, says,

"Everyone, I lost the belt that was around my waist. It has pockets full of small survival gear in them."

Everyone stops to look down the steps. Nothing is on the steps. They decide to keep climbing upward.

A few minutes later, they arrive at the top of the steps while out of breath. They're all reaching for their canteens to drink water. Giao is actually in the best shape of all of them.

"That wasn't that bad," says Giao.

"Try lugging food and water up those steps 20 times a day. That's what the old monks who lived here used to do," says Cisco.

"I think I just saw one of them," remarks Giao as he thinks of the old man he saw sitting at the top of the steps.

"This place has memories, Your Majesty," says Jada.
"Yes, memories we can actually see," responds Giao.

They're standing on the front stone plaza area several feet from a large arched entrance doorway. The doorway is about 20 feet tall and 10 feet wide. It has no actual doors and is pitch black beyond the threshold. Cisco throws down his bag and pulls out some high-tech lanterns each person either holds, straps on their arms, or drapes around their necks. They proceed to walk inside with their lanterns turned on.

❖ CHAPTER SEVEN ❖

The lanterns are lighting up a large entrance gallery 34 daradems cubed in size (49 meters or 159 feet). The ancient priesthoods were minimalists and purists. They believed there is a universal language in proportionality whose geometric forms are determined by how well matter resonates with an original source singularity of consciousness. This function of measurement and determination in nature forms a spectrum out of which all the forms arise and repeat throughout nature. It's nature self-organizing. The forms compose a *Sacred Geometry.*

The self-organizing force is called, *Alpha.* Alpha is the operating force of the law of sympathetic vibrations or sympathetic resonance. When matter and consciousness are brought into resonance, Alpha emerges to reorganize that matter into a new matrix to sustain the new level of resonance between the two. It is the underlying alchemy of the universe. It's through this operation that all the geometric forms arise. Cymatics studies the wave formations of sympathetic vibrations.

The ancient priesthood sought discovery of these forms. They built their structures using these forms to aid the human mind in communing with the source. The forms are unlimited, although recognized innately by a mind which is truly *awake.* A mind is considered awake when it is free to commune with the forces of consciousness underlying creation uninhibited by the inherited autonomic programs of the mind passed down through human evolution. The ancient priesthoods called these underlying forces of consciousness the *Cosmic Quanta.*

Examples of these forms are, the Golden Ratio within the famous Fibonacci Sequence, the ratio of Pi, the Flower of Life, Fractals, Metatron's Cube, the Hexagon, the Trinity, and much more.

In the pitch-black darkness of the gallery, Cisco says, "I have been here twice before, Giao. The building is sleeping. We need to wake it up and let it know we are here."

Giao turns and looks at Cisco with a perplexed expression. Cisco points down to a carved groove in the stone floor.

"We have to follow this line," explains Cisco.

They follow the line about 20 feet to a stone pylon with geometric carvings. Among the stone carvings, there's a protruding node.

"Giao, push the stone in front of you," says Cisco.

Looking down a bit, Giao finds the node and pushes on it with his hand. With one push the node continues inward on its own.

As the node becomes flush with the wall, a loud thumping sound starts permeating the gallery as a multitude of giant stone pilasters along the perimeter begin moving outward, allowing outside light into the gallery. The beams of light coming in through the perimeter wall are directed toward a giant crystal monolith standing at the center of the gallery spanning from floor to ceiling. The crystal absorbs the light, amplifies it, and sends it right back out into the room in all directions to light up the gallery at a level of brightness ten times that of the outside. The dim red glow of the outside light has been transformed into a bright soft yellow light, and with no synthetic technology.

The Orion were masters at getting large megalithic stone structures to function like sophisticated machines with nothing but stone, water, light, air, gravity, crystals, and harmonic resonance.

At the same time the gallery is lighting up, a soothing breeze of fresh air begins circulating throughout the gallery induced by a manipulation of air pressure via the movement of the stones.

Just as everyone in the group is busy looking around in amazement, a tall, willowy, slender man with an elongated bald head and strands of white hair drooping down from the sides of his head walks out of a dark doorway from across the room into the gallery to greet everyone. He's wearing a one-piece black robe with a white turtleneck shirt underneath. He has no beard and his skin is pale white. He has some similar facial features, but he doesn't look like other Orion with his elongated skull and lack of blue pigment in his skin.

The old man gets everyone's attention as he walks up to them with his hands folded together in front and an inquisitive look on his face.

"Welcome, my name is Shenzu. What brings you here today?" Cisco moves out from behind Ann and says,

"Shenzu, it's me, Cisco. Remember, I was here two years ago with a group of scientists? We stayed for two days and one night. We were supposed to stay longer, but the scientists suddenly cut their trip short."

"Ah, yes, Cisco. I remember you. What brings you back today?" asks Shenzu.

"Shenzu, please allow me to introduce you to His Majesty, Chief Justice, Lord Giao Setairius of the royal family," says Cisco as he points at Giao. Giao steps up and nods his head slightly to Shenzu.

"Your Majesty, please forgive me for not recognizing you. The temple is honored by your presence. I am at your service," says Shenzu.

"The honor is mine, Shenzu. I am not here in any official capacity. I am here only out of personal interest. Please, just call me Giao like my other friends here with us today," says Giao as he points to Ann, Hector, Jada and Cisco.

"As you wish, Giao. What is your matter of personal interest?" asks Shenzu.

"I wish to study the ancient manuscripts in this temple's library," answers Giao.

"Ah! Of course! I can assist you with that. How long will you be staying?" asks Shenzu.

"We will be staying tonight and tomorrow night," answers Giao.

"Very well. Just a couple of things. We have no lavatories or facilities for cooking, cleaning, sleeping, or bathing. It's no different than camp. Are you prepared for that?"

"Yes, Shenzu, we have camp gear and food for everyone. We will leave everything exactly the way we found it. Nothing will be left behind," says Jada.

"Perfect. Cisco, I suggest you sleep in the same chambers you and the others slept in the last time. Do you remember how to get there?"

"Yes, Shenzu, I remember. The East Chambers," says Cisco. Giao interjects.

"Shenzu, if you don't mind, can you take me to the library now? We don't have much time to waste. Cisco, just come and find me in a few hours in the library," says Giao.

"Certainly, Giao. I will take you there now," says Shenzu.

"While Giao is doing that, Hector and I will start conducting our scientific investigations," announces Ann.

"Excellent, Cisco and I will go set up camp for everyone inside the East Chambers," says Jada.

The group heads in different directions leaving Giao and Shenzu.

"Right this way, Giao," says Shenzu as they begin walking across the big open gallery.

Giao is admiring the illuminated crystal as he follows Shenzu. The crystal is primarily white with hues of silver and hints of gold.

They're beyond the entrance gallery walking through a grand corridor formed by massive stones on either side curving upward at the top to touch and form an arch. It looks like a series of large ribs.

"Shenzu, if you don't mind me asking, of what humanity are you a member? I haven't seen the likes of you before," says Giao.

"I'm Orion," says Shenzu.

"But you don't look Orion," exclaims Giao.

"I'm over 10,000 years old. I am the last surviving member of the Barstow humanoid genetic program, a program conducted long ago to modify the Orion genome to thrive within Barstow's unique ecology.

"The program was abruptly terminated and Barstow and Jenesis declared forbidden worlds by King Leer, your grandfather," says Shenzu.

"That's incredible, Shenzu. You must hold a wealth of knowledge. I would love to get to know you better and learn about your history," says Giao as he looks over at Shenzu with fascination.

"Indeed. There is no shortage of historians knocking at my door. I've fully debriefed several over the years. I've shared everything, both the good and the bad. It's a shame that my kind was not allowed to continue. We had some unique abilities which were never fully explored in pursuit of a scientific understanding of the human condition. Instead, we were considered freaks of nature and quarantined here on this forbidden world," says Shenzu.

"What kind of abilities, Shenzu?" asks Giao.

"Well, for one, I can remember everything. Every conversation I ever had with anyone I remember word for word. I also do complex math problems in my mind instantaneously," says Shenzu.

"That is actually quite strange," says Giao

They both burst out laughing.

"Why did they stop your kind from developing further," asks Giao. "We were declared psychopathic. One side of our brain over developed to the determinant of our emotional faculties. And they were not wrong. I have never cried or grieved once in all my existence. I'm essentially an organic android," explains Shenzu.

"We probably have some traits in common, Shenzu. I too, believe it or not, am an outcast," says Giao.

After walking through the big corridor and turning a couple of times down smaller ancillary halls, they arrive inside a circular antechamber five daradems (7 meters / 23 feet) in diameter with a glowing illumination on the floor. Giao looks up to see the inside of a tall stone cylindrical spire stretching beyond the eyes can see with light cascading downward from reflecting crystals expertly placed throughout the interior of the spire to push light down into the antechamber below. Giao looks at a wall with intricate stone carvings of sacred geometric forms with a white light washing down over them.

Shenzu pushes on a stone node protruding from the wall. A section of the wall immediately begins moving upward to reveal a doorway into the library beyond. The opening of the door causes various stone blocks inside the library to move allowing light into its large chamber. This light is then amplified and disbursed by a ceiling full of crystals. Suddenly, it's as bright as day inside the library. The library chamber is 55 daradems square (79 meters / 254 feet) with polished emerald-green stone cubicle shelving, 2' deep, at the perimeter spanning floor to ceiling. The white crystal ceiling is ten daradems in height (14 meters / 47 feet). Inside the cubes are thousands of manuscripts rolled up inside tubes engineered to protect the contents accessed by wood ladders on rollers.

The middle of the room has large wood timber tables and benches to sit at and study the manuscripts. Shenzu and Giao step inside the library. Giao looks up at the perimeter shelving holding thousands of scrolls.

"Giao, perhaps if you tell me what you are looking for, I can help you find it," says Shenzu.

"Do you have an index system?" asks Giao.

"Yes, I maintain a master index scroll of every scroll's location in the library, but that's more for when I die. I don't need the index. I know the subject and location of every scroll by memory," says Shenzu.

"That's incredible, Shenzu. You are strange indeed. Have you read and put to memory all of the scrolls?" asks Giao. Shenzu replies,

"No, actually, I've read only very few of the scrolls. Most of them were written in the ancient second kingdom Orionis language which I never had the technology to translate. Nor was anyone allowed to translate the manuscripts for fear of mistranslations. The old caretaker monks were authorized to at least translate the subject matter and record that information on the master index scroll."

"Well, I'm a member of the royal family of the Orion Empire and I just so happen to have these," says Giao while holding up his pair of reading glasses which can translate the manuscripts in conjunction with the universal translator chip embedded behind his ear. Giao continues,

"By all of the authority invested in me by His Majesty, the King, to serve as the Chief Justice of the Supreme Court of all Orion worlds, I hereby authorize that I can use these reading glasses to translate the manuscripts so they can be deciphered."

"Well, I guess that settles that! Now that that's out of the way, let's get down to business. What is the subject matter, Giao?" asks Shenzu.

"The subject matter is the creation of the universe and its firstborn as well any reference to there being any form of awareness embedded within matter itself," answers Giao.

"Aha, we have 11 manuscripts that deal with the process of creation. More manuscripts may mention creation and the nature of matter within its content, but I wouldn't know," says Shenzu.

"Excellent! Would you mind retrieving those eleven manuscripts for me, Shenzu?" asks Giao

"Certainly, Sir," answers Shenzu as he begins climbing a ladder to retrieve the first manuscript.

Meanwhile, in the East Chambers, Jada and Cisco are setting up camp for everyone. Each person has their own room to sleep inside. The rooms are lined along the perimeter of a circle. At the inner center of the circle is a community area where two perpendicular corridors meet to intersect and the team can gather for a meal. A tall spire rises above the inner circle cascading light into the area.

Cisco is busy setting a fire in the community center circle with charcoals and a kettle over top of the fire. The center of the inner circle is made of firestones darkened over thousands of years of use.

The spire above creates an air vacuum pulling the smoke from the fire upward high into its chamber and out the sides of the spire where light is allowed through. While Cisco is busy with the fire, Jada walks out from one of the rooms holding a lantern whose light has turned off.

"Cisco, this lantern is not working. It started to blink and then faded out," says Jada as she taps the lantern a couple of times.

Cisco grabs the lantern to check it. A second later, he looks up at Jada while holding it in his hands and says,

"Jada, nothing ever seems to work in this place. The last time I used fully charged battery-operated lanterns. They died minutes after entering the cathedral. This time I brought lanterns which run directly off the zero-point-energy vacuum. Even these don't work."

Minutes later, as Hector is roaming the cathedral with an electric monitoring device, it begins going haywire. While he's looking down at the device flashing all kinds of hieroglyphics, he hears a clamoring of voices of an eerie otherworldly nature. Hector walks 20 more feet and hears it again. This time he can decipher the words, "Get out!"

Back in the library, Shenzu is at the top of one of the ladder's pulling out a tube in a cubicle near the top of the shelving.

Giao is busy reading a manuscript with his reading glasses on from the first tube Shenzu brought him.

Suddenly, Giao's reading glasses fly off his face and land on the table in front of him. Giao picks up the glasses to keep reading, but he pauses to think about how his glasses flew off his face so weirdly.

The lights in the library dim for a minute and then return to their full brightness. Shenzu is walking up to Giao with another tube.

"Shenzu, a moment ago, did you see the lights dim and then go back up again?" asks Giao."

"Yes, Sir, sometimes that happens because of the passing clouds. It takes a minute for the crystals to redistribute the light," says Shenzu.

"Ah! Okay, that makes sense," says Giao as he keeps reading.

"Giao, here are the remainder of the manuscripts. I will go now and check on the others. I will come back later," says Shenzu.

"Okay, Shenzu. Thank you for your assistance. I will see you later," says Giao as he continues with his head down in concentration.

Giao perused the first two manuscripts but found the third manuscript much more interesting. It tells the story of creation via a metaphorical tale. The one passage below strikes him.

And she rises from the virons of the deep in a primordial chaos before all other things are made. From her body, all things are fashioned. She is the first, the last, and the one who is many. Her spirit moves in the soils of the land as the serpent. Wise and wicked, she is the Kiraphon.

Giao pushes back from the manuscript, startled by the passage. Just as he does this, a tube flies across the room from out of the shelving. He stands up and walks slowly toward the tube and picks it up.

A stirring shadow catches Giao's eye at the far-left corner of the room. He suddenly realizes there is a narrow space between where the shelving is supposed to intersect and meet but does not.

He reaches back to place the tube on the timber table behind him while his eyes remain fixed on the dark space at the corner of the room. As he steps toward the dark corner, Giao's heart is thumping.

The dark open corner is only a couple of feet wide. It's a narrow passage. With bated breath, Giao decides to step inside.

There's a dim light rising from a four feet wide staircase. Giao takes one step down the stairs and suddenly he's hanging from the edge with a deep chasm void below him. The stairs are gone. Zombie-like beings are trying to pull Giao down while wailing and gnashing their teeth. Suddenly, Raiden is at the top of the stairs trying to pull Giao up.

Giao falls into oblivion with Raiden receding from view.

The Gorgon appears in the darkness in a long black dress with long silver hair flowing out from her head like snakes moving in the wind. She has the same exotic face as when they first met on the Grid.

The Gorgon says, "Do not fear the darkness, Giao. I'm your champion. Allow me to rise and fight your battles. I will win. Through me, you will attain everything.

"Come to meee, Come to meee, Come to meee."

Giao wakes up startled at the table like having fallen from above. He's in a cold sweat. He looks at the written passage one more time.

He touches his glasses to snap a picture of it. He then remembers the flying tube. He looks, and there is no extra tube on the table.

He gets up to walk around the table to inspect the far corner of the room. Sure enough, there's a dark narrow passage. Giao sticks his head in to look around. Instead of seeing steps, he sees an old blocked-up opening in the floor. Tap, tap, on his shoulder. Giao spins around. "Oh my God! Shenzu! You scared the hell out of me," exclaims Giao.

"I'm sorry, Sir. I had no intention of that," says Shenzu.

"It's quite alright. I'm glad you are here. Tell me something, Shenzu. Why is there a blocked opening in the floor here?" asks Giao.

"That was done out of respect for the dead," answers Shenzu. "The dead! What are you talking about, Shenzu?" questions Giao.

"Giao, below that blocked opening is a set of steps leading down into the catacombs. In the catacombs lies the bodies of all the monks who once lived in the cathedral. The catacombs are under the library. They wanted to be near their scriptures. It's a monk's life's work.

"Shenzu, I found what I was looking for in the scriptures. Our business is done here. You have been a tremendous help to me. Is there anything that I can do for you?" asks Giao.

"No, Sir, I have everything I need here," says Shenzu.

"Oh, wait. There is one thing, peaches from Erawan. I had them once. I have dreamed of them ever since," says Shenzu.

"I will take care of that," says Giao with a smile as he touches Shenzu's shoulder.

"Right this way, Sir. I will take you to your team," says Shenzu.

After walking down a few corridors, they arrive at the rotunda area of the East Chambers to find Hector, Jada, and Cisco wrapping a bandage around Ann's lower leg. Surprised, Giao asks,

"What happened, Ann?"

"I don't know. It's really strange. I was walking around taking measurements with my device when I looked down and I was bleeding. I must have cut myself somewhere and didn't realize it," says Ann.

"All, it's time to leave. I found what I needed. We shouldn't stay here a minute longer than we need to," says Giao.

Everyone is relieved and in agreement. They say their farewells to Shenzu and quickly leave the Cathedral. As they're making their way down the steps, Giao turns and looks back up to see the same old monk with a long white beard in the same position watching them leave.

They make it back to the shuttle without incident. Ann was able to reach Hal through the Equinox who quickly returned to take them back to Erawan station, where they all parted ways. Giao did make sure, however, to send Shenzu a crate of Erawan peaches.

The events on Barstow didn't encourage Lord Giao to experiment with the Omicron cortical node again. Just the opposite, they made him want to return to the life he had and forget everything, and for the next six months, that's exactly what he did. He focused on his court cases and tried to think about the Gorgon as little as possible.

CHAPTER EIGHT

BEYOND REM-ONKOR

Solemn, vast, and timeless appears space, the progeny of nous. Quintessentials, noumenalities, causalities, sing a song sung in illuminating rhapsody to reveal an entirely different melody. An omniverse of correlated points washing away countless infinitudes. A boundless churning sea of incalculable potentialities realized but in a single instant. An ineffable choir rising from an empty space of strings. A matrix unfathomable, but in song, all together one.

After its brief rendezvous with the Tau Orionis, the Valkyrie is moving quickly through the Bellatrix star system surfing the outer gas giants on its way to the inner sanctum of the Orion terrestrial domain when it comes upon Planet Leer, a mysterious and majestic blue world. They're heading straight toward the northern hemisphere to touch the face of the august realm when suddenly they pick up speed rising swiftly above its arctic pole into the blazing radiance of the Bellatrix sun.

Now cruising near the speed of light, the Valkyrie arcs right into the darkness of space when ship monitors announce Artep is straight ahead. Lord Raiden is sitting alongside Zeina as he hails his father and brother. Both Lord Giao and King Sah answer Raiden's call on the viewscreen. Lord Giao is preparing for court in his chambers at the Orion Ministry. King Sah is outside at the royal villa with the countryside in the rear.

"Father, brother, I'm in the new Valkyrie *en route* to Planet Artep. We should arrive there in the next few minutes. As you already know, the anomaly on Artep is believed to be a hyperspace portal left behind by the Anthro-Orionis. The next stage of the investigation will be an experiment to send an artificial human through the aperture.

"We've selected Chief Engineer Royce Allen of the Betelgeuse. Zeina and her team are assuming command of the operation. Being that this is potentially a historically significant event, you are both invited to observe the experiment on Planet Artep," says Raiden.

"Raiden, thank you for the update. I would love to be there. I will start making my way there now," says King Sah.

"I will be there as well, Raiden. In accordance with protocol, Father and I will be arriving on two separate shuttles," says Giao.

The Valkyrie is fast approaching the Artep system of celestial worlds as its brilliant violet, white, and blue sphere emerges into view. As the ship leans left into a circular orbital approach, the lunar body, Ursa, one of Artep's three sister moons, begins gleaming on the horizon. It's mostly a rocky, barren, cratered world with a faint blue atmosphere. Zeina is steering the Valkyrie to the underside of Ursa's southern pole. The cratered world is now rolling above the Valkyrie with the bridge in full transparent mode. It looks like you can almost reach up and touch the moon while passing below its lunar terrain.

The Valkyrie is entering orbit around Artep behind the Atlas. By Orion security rules, the ship is too large to enter the atmosphere. Teleporting down to the surface or to its underworld cities is strictly forbidden, even for the royal family. Raiden, Zeina, and Royce will be taking a shuttle to the Ingersoll Marine Facility from the Valkyrie, but they're waiting for the King and Chief Justice to arrive. Maia and Kurzon are staying aboard the Valkyrie to work remotely with the team.

Two imperial shuttles from Planet Erawan are arriving behind a fleet of Orion military vessels. Lord Raiden's shuttle disembarks the Valkyrie with Zeina and Royce on board to lead the two imperial shuttles carrying Lord Giao and King Sah down to the marine facility. They're taking the same route Doctor Crane had taken into the mountain, across the underworld city, and through the hyperloop transit system.

Everyone has arrived and are walking together down the same corridors of the facility the Doctor had walked with Captain Miles Garran. They enter the command center. Qurel Song, Miles Garran, Ethan Decker and the 12 scientists, including Doctor Elden Crane, are standing at attention for Lord Raiden, Lord Giao, King Sah and their entourage as they walk through the door.

Qurel Song takes the lead directing everyone to their chairs in front of the big screen. After initial pleasantries and introductions, Qurel provides a brief historical recap leading up to the current meeting. He then proceeds into an explanation of what they are about to attempt next.

Qurel is speaking,

"That brings us to what the study group will attempt to do next. The next logical step is to send something intelligent through the aperture; something sentient and self-aware; something that could improvise on the other side and hopefully find its way back to us.

"Simple probes cannot do this. The study group recommends sending an artificial humanoid being. This is proposed not because we value artificial beings any less than organic beings, but because in many ways, artificial beings are superior, and we want to leverage their superior abilities in such a high-stakes scientific investigation.

"Another advantage an artificial humanoid has over an organic lifeform is we can back up its mind, a risky procedure which is against Orion law. This law exists to prevent the systemic abuse of a conscious living mind. Lord Raiden has made a special exception in this case."

Raiden and Giao look at each other, but both are in agreement. Qurel continues.

"We have chosen Chief Engineer Royce Allen of the Betelgeuse to enter the aperture. Royce has accepted the mission along with its risks. Captain Zeina Bellatrix of Betelgeuse, Royce's commanding officer, has taken command of this operation. Captain Miles Garran of the Atlas and Lieutenant Commander Ethan Decker of the Maricrisodon will continue under the command of Captain Zeina Bellatrix. The mission which discovered the anomaly, *Operation Ocean Horizon*, is hereby concluded. We now officially begin *Operation Jump Shot*."

Qurel walks away. Zeina walks up and begins speaking.

"At 07:00 hours this morning I officially assumed operational command of Operation Jump Shot. While still on the Betelgeuse in the Aldebaran, I was fully debriefed by Captain Garran and Lieutenant Commander Decker. By special authorization, Euclid, one of our greatest cybernetic engineers, was given the critical task of backing up the cybernetic mind of Chief Engineer Royce Allen.

"Euclid has just joined us here in conference," says Zeina as she points over to Euclid who is standing at the side of the room in attention.

Zeina continues.

"The majesty's study team, in cooperation with Captain Garran and Lt. Commander Decker, developed a few different approaches on how to send Chief Royce Allen through the aperture. Their recommended approach is to send the Maricrisodon through the aperture with only Chief Allen onboard. Royce and I agree, but with one exception.

"We will send Royce through the aperture. But not with the Maricrisodon. We will send Royce aboard the Valkyrie," declares Zeina.

People are stirring in the room after hearing this announcement. There's a look of curiosity from Raiden and raised eyebrows from Ethan.

"Raiden, I'm sorry. I know the Valkyrie is your new prized ship, but Royce deserves the best we have. The Maricrisodon is a fine ship Ethan, but she pales in comparison to the Valkyrie," says Zeina.

"Zeina, I support your decision. We have the blueprints. We can always rebuild the Valkyrie. But Royce, if you destroy the Valkyrie, I think you will hold the record for the shortest time someone ever had a new starship before they destroyed it." says Raiden.

Ethan settles down after Raiden's comment.

Royce chimes in with his typical matter-of-fact voice.

"You are correct, Sir. I would take the record. Currently, Captain Jared Bates holds the record after being the Captain of the Alnitak-C for only two days, 12 hours and 32 minutes before it was lost in the battle of Kinnib in the Minizet wars 43 years ago."

"Really? I will have to talk with Jared about that," remarks Raiden.

Zeina continues.

"Although the Maricrisodon and the Valkyrie are similar in size, they are two completely different types of vessels. The Valkyrie will need to pass through the aperture tilted 90 degrees to clear the width. The aperture is 221 daradems in height (+/- 317 meters / 1,040 feet) and only about 17 daradems in total width (+/- 24 meters / 80 feet). We will utilize the Atlas to teleport the Valkyrie from orbit around Artep to the inside of the Rem-Onkor Cavern. From that point forward, Chief Allen will pilot the Valkyrie through the aperture event horizon. The only major task remaining to complete before we can proceed is to back up Chief Allen's cybernetic neuro-matrix."

After Zeina completed her explanation, Doctor Crane spoke and raised his concern about what happens if first contact is made with a new intelligent lifeform such as the Anthro-Orionis. Royce answered and said he would follow the Orion protocols already established for first contact. However, the study group recommended, and King Sah authorized, that they revisit that protocol while Royce and Euclid worked on backing up Royce's cybernetic neuro-matrix.

Euclid approaches Royce and says in a straight-forward monotone voice,

"Chief Royce Allen, under emergency orders authorized by the Chancellor of the Pleiadean Science Academy, Qurel Song, and His Majesty, King Sah, we have modified the parameters of the science academy's latest cybernetic human android initiative, *Project CyOps 9.* We decided to utilize its cybernetic organism to back up your mind. It has not yet been animated, making such an alteration possible.

"Ethically, it is only proper to back up your sentient mind to a cybernetic organism more advanced than what you currently possess. This way, if Project Jump Shot were to fail, you would wake up inside a more evolved cybernetic lifeform, rather than inside of some computer console all alone in the back corner of a laboratory."

Royce responds.

"Doctor Kyle Euclid, or as you prefer, Euclid, I wish to convey my gratitude. I was somewhat concerned that I would wake up inside a box. The academy has proven to have always looked out for my best interests. My trust is confirmed once again. Although I don't have a single progenitor who I could point to and call father or mother, doctors such as yourself have served just as well."

"I understand and appreciate your sentiments, Royce. We are there for each other. You officially now have two bodies, although you have not yet met your new twin body. I have your new twin body aboard my ship in stasis waiting for the procedure. My ship, *the Mentat*, is in orbit around Artep. Shall we go now?" asks Euclid as he points the way.

Euclid and Royce inform Zeina and Qurel they are on their way to the Mentat to perform the procedure and that Royce will return with the Valkyrie according to plan. Afterward, Euclid will head to the Betelgeuse to assist with the fleet upgrades on Royce's behalf.

While *en route* to the Mentat, Royce and Euclid continue their conversation about the procedure Royce is about to undergo.

"Euclid, I have been following the scientific journals on CyOps 9. There's been a lot of controversy over the project," comments Royce.

"This is true, Royce. Several high-ranking scientists on the academy's cybernetic board contend that CyOps 9 is too advanced and poses too high a risk to the social order. They fear such a sentient being would be godlike in comparison to most other sentient life," says Euclid.

"And yet there are so many basic human traits we still lack, Euclid, such as humor. Humor is something I honestly struggle with every day. And granted, CyOp sevens and eights have proven to be citizens who are more ethically reliable than organics, but only because it's a moral ethos encoded into our prime neural matrix to safeguard organics from synthetics. I wonder how much of myself is driven by a computer code, versus driven by an awareness arising out of the underlying quantum field to generate the phenomenon we call consciousness," says Royce.

Euclid thinks for a moment and then responds,

"Synthetics endeavor to self-actualize just as organics do, Royce. We are set to evolve. I believe synthetics and organics support each other's evolution. In tandem, one never gets too far ahead of the other. If the CyOps 9 program places people outside of their comfort zones, so much the better. It will compel the organic side of life to catch up to rebalance the equation. We evolve through challenge and adversity. The synthetic side of life is a mirror to the organic side of life and vice versa. We are symbiotic," says Euclid.

Euclid and Royce make their way through the hyperloop system and take a shuttle into orbit around Artep. They're now approaching the Mentat, a cybernetic android ship built by androids for androids. It looks Orion with its sleek black windowless triangular design, but the ship lacks chairs and human life-support systems. It has alcoves for recharging. It doesn't even have a front viewscreen. The androids inside the ship see what the ship sees. They're an extension of the ship.

The interior of the Mentat is minimalistic and utilitarian by design. Strangely, the inside is mostly a geometric maze of corridors with only a few small rooms. In cross-section, the maze looks like a cerebral cortex. The walls of the maze function as an interactive computer interface.

❖ BEYOND REM-ONKOR ❖

Now inside the Mentat, Euclid and Royce are walking through the geometric maze of interconnecting corridors with no signage or way-finding devices. Organics would get lost in a second. Every corner has a rounded edge. Every wall has the same light beige-colored panel which can instantly transform into an interactive computer interface. All the ceilings are white with a light alcove running horizontally between the ceiling and wall. The floor is made of a glossy super-durable white resin material. For organics, the Mentat is too cool for comfort and the place is immaculately clean. The androids on the ship have no private quarters to call their own. There are no meeting rooms, no galleys, no bathrooms, no observatories. All they have are corridors, a few small rooms, and recharging alcoves sunk inside the corridors which disappear when they're not being used. At first, the simplicity and minimalism are praiseworthy, but after five minutes, it becomes amazingly dull and repetitive, just the way androids like it.

Actually, there is one small area of the ship reserved for organics if they ever have them aboard. It has all the essential amenities needed by organics, but this small corner of the ship is seldom utilized.

Euclid and Royce arrive at one of the small rooms. It has a three-foot-wide all-glass cylinder with a naked man standing inside sleeping.

"Royce 8, meet Royce 9," says Euclid.

Royce is quietly examining his surrogate twin inside the tube and says,

"If I die and wake up as him, I will use a new name. We don't look like twins. By organic standards, Mr. 9 is more handsome," says Royce.

Euclid begins typing on a blank wall which immediately transforms into a computer screen. The glass cylinder starts slowly spinning around to reveal a second location inside the cylinder so both Royce 8 and Royce 9 can stand back-to-back.

"I know on the Betelgeuse, and most ships of the 12 Orion fleets, people utilize the OHMN Com neuro link to communicate. Ironically, here on the Mentat, while we certainly have this capability, we prefer not to use it. Not using it gives us the only sense of privacy we ever get, and it reaffirms our individuality, something we androids are always having to fight for. So, that's how we designed the ship. We can all instantly act as one, or we can stay separate and function as distinct individuals. It's a dynamic cellular architecture," says Euclid.

"I love the ship, Euclid. I feel at peace here," says Royce as he gets inside the glass cylinder facing away from the CyOps 9 android.

"My sentiments exactly, Royce," says Euclid as he attaches a pulsing cable of light between the back of Royce's head with the back of the CyOps 9 head.

Royce was contemplating what Euclid had said about how the ship was designed to function. He responds,

"And that's just another dichotomy between organics and synthetics, Euclid. Organics strive every day to learn how to better function together as one harmonious mind via systems like the Orion Com, while we synthetics, who are already masters at acting as one, endeavor every day to discover our individuality. They want to become more like us, and we want to become like them," says Royce as the light pulses back and forth between him and his surrogate.

"There is a poetic irony to it, Royce," says Euclid.

Euclid steps away from Royce as he types away on a different wall panel with lightning-fast speed. He then steps back toward Royce, opens a door to his chest cavity, and connects another device.

Royce looks down with a perplexed expression and says, "How did I not know about that inter-plexus point, Euclid?" asks Royce.

"We don't want androids tinkering with the neurosynaptic pathways governing the super cognitive functions of what one may call the soul. We certainly want you to use it. We just don't want you tinkering with its interconnectivity like I'm doing now. It operates on a quantum level in several dimensions simultaneously. If it gets entangled in the wrong manner, it cannot be corrected. You would die. Now you are aware of it, and with that knowledge comes a new level of responsibility," says Euclid.

Euclid continues talking while working on Royce.

"It requires someone with my knowledge and expertise to work on the *Quantumplex* as we call it. The quantumplex is constantly evolving, updating, and rewriting itself based on your experiences, knowledge, and realizations. It's what allows an android to self-actualize. It gives you a sense of self and allows you to form a personality and remember who you are. It's what we want to save in case the Valkyrie is destroyed. We will also save your memories and knowledge, but your memories and knowledge alone do not form your essence," explains Euclid.

In a voice altered to imitate organics, Royce says,
"That's some deep stuff, dude!"

Euclid pauses with an odd expression to look up at Royce.
After a second of pause, they both let out a big laugh.

"You did it, Royce! That's humor!" says Euclid.

"I bet you thought you messed something up," says Royce with a smile.

"You got me. For a second, I was a little concerned," says Euclid.

Euclid twitches his neck and is now working on the inside of the same chest cavity on the Royce 9 android as he was with Royce 8. He's using a second device identical to what is still mounted to Royce's chest cavity. Each device is blinking to a different rhythm.

Euclid is now holding a third device in his hands as he keeps intermittently tapping quickly with his fingers like playing a musical instrument. He's tapping away on the device for a couple of minutes. The rhythmic light patterns on all three devices are now blinking together in harmonic unison.

Euclid stops and says,

"Your two bodies are now conjoined. If you lose one body, you can still use the other."

Euclid touches the back of the neck of Royce 9 who immediately opens his eyes to stare out into a blank space.

Royce 8 and Royce 9 begin speaking together in unison,

"Thank you, Doctor Euclid. I will take care to maintain both cybernetic organisms in pursuit of realizing my ultimate potential."

Royce 8 and Royce 9, mirroring each other's every move, turn in unison to look at each other with curiosity.

Euclid touches the back of Royce 9's neck again to put him back to sleep inside the glass cylinder. He's now detaching all the devices.

"That's it, Royce. We're finished. You are now cleared to proceed with Operation Jump Shot.

"Euclid, again, my gratitude," says Royce with a respectful nod.

"It is certainly my pleasure, Royce. I will be heading to the Betelgeuse now to serve in your position while you're on your mission with the Valkyrie," says Euclid.

Royce is now standing at attention in the middle of the room. He nods at Euclid and then disappears as he teleports to the Valkyrie.

Royce materializes on the bridge of the Valkyrie to find Maia and Kurzon waiting for him.

"Maia, Kurzon, greetings. I only have a few minutes to prepare for the teleportation of the Valkyrie to the Rem Onkor Ocean Cavern," says Royce as he walks toward the captain's chair. Maia responds,

"We've already been debriefed, Royce. Kurzon and I have been preparing the Valkyrie for the teleportation to the deep ocean cavern. It's ready for immersion into the Permian underwater environment. Once you signal *when*, Kurzon and I will beam to the Atlas."

Kurzon walks over to Royce with a device in her hand and starts scanning him and says,

"Royce, I just want to confirm that nothing was inadvertently altered by Euclid."

"A wise precaution, Kurzon," says Royce.
The scanning device is finished. Kurzon is reading the results.

"Everything checks out, Royce. Oddly some of your autonomic systems are functioning at a notably higher efficiency than three days ago when I last checked you," says Kurzon with a surprised expression.

As Royce is typing away at the side console, he responds,

"Yes, I am aware of that, Kurzon. My CyOps 8 organism is in symbiotic parity with my CyOps 9 organism which operates at an even higher efficiency than what you are currently reading on your device. The parity is bootstrapping my CyOps 8 organism to a higher level."

"That, Royce, is extraordinary," says Kurzon as she walks away. Royce hails Zeina who is sitting with Raiden, Qurel, and Doctor Crane. A transparent screen appears before the four with Royce on the screen.

"Captain, I'm aboard the Valkyrie. The procedure with Doctor Euclid was successful. I now have two cybernetic organisms locked in quantum neuronetic symbiosis. My essence now exists in two places at once. Doctor Euclid is already on his way to the Betelgeuse aboard the Mentat. Maia and Kurzon are here helping me prepare the Valkyrie before they leave for the Atlas," says Royce.

"Excellent, Royce. The Atlas is ready and is standing by to teleport the Valkyrie at your command," says Zeina.

"Royce, the study team and I went through the protocols for first contact if it should happen. We made some modifications. We're transmitting the latest protocol to you now," says Doctor Crane.

Raiden wishes to lighten the tension in the air and says,

"Royce, when you finish this mission, Elden, Zeina, and my brother Giao will join us for a game of QauZu."

"Excellent, Your Majesty. Organics are so unpredictable. It's one of the few games where organics and synthetics are on equal footing. I hear your brother is quite a challenge. I look forward to it," says Royce.

King Sah and Lord Giao walk up while they're talking to Royce. Giao squeezes in between Raiden and Zeina to see Royce and says,

"Royce, the Tribunal Overlord of Intergalactic affairs officially declares a QauZu challenge to the Principate of Cybernetic Worlds."

Royce sits up in the captain's chair and pulls down his shirt to make a more formal and proper pose. He then replies,

"The challenge is accepted, Your Majesty."
King Shah chimes in,

"Royce, if you beat Giao in QauZu, I'll make sure it's recorded in the history books."

Someone comes up and whispers in Qurel's ear. Qurel then interrupts the conversation and says,

"Everyone, we need to move forward and begin. We just entered the optimal window for teleport based on various planetary and solar factors. We're dropping the Artep security field in 5 minutes."

As soon as Qurel says this, Royce says,
"Zeina, the Valkyrie will be ready in four minutes. I will see you on the other side. Royce out."

"Maia and Kurzon, it's time for you and any other remaining crew members to leave the Valkyrie," says Royce.

"Only Kurzon and I are left on board. Have a safe trip, Royce," says Maia as she and Kurzon wave goodbye.

Royce gives them his farewell nod from the captain's chair as they both dematerialize on their way to the Atlas.

Royce hails the Atlas,

"Atlas, this is Chief Royce Allen of the Valkyrie. The ship is ready for teleportation to the Rem-Onkor Ocean Cavern."

"Chief Royce Allen, this is Lieutenant Commander Ethan Decker aboard the Atlas. The Artep security field is down. We're initiating the Valkyrie teleportation sequence, T-mark two minutes and counting. M now has sequence control," says Ethan.

Everyone in the marine facility and aboard the three ships is watching large viewscreens split into two screens. One side shows the Valkyrie in orbit around Artep. The other side shows video footage being shot by the Maricrisodon of the area inside the Rem-Onkor Ocean Cavern where the Valkyrie is set to be teleported. It shows an ocean basin of pristine blue water with a deep cavern floor below sparkling with pure white sand clear of any vegetation.

M is providing updates to everyone in all four locations including the Marine Facility, the Valkyrie, the Maricrisodon, and the Atlas,

"Valkyrie, we are in teleport countdown T-minus one minute and counting. Please be seated and ready to energize."

Royce is calmly watching his viewscreen tapping his fingers on his side console in a repeating pattern.

Lieutenant Maia Elsu is aboard the Atlas checking instrument readings on her forward-command console.

M speaks again,

"T-minus ten seconds and counting. All systems are functional and proceeding on silent countdown."

The viewscreens in each location show the countdown. The time is running down, five, four, three, two, one.

Suddenly, an incredibly bright light begins filling the screens while an oscillating vibration noise builds to a crescendo for several seconds and then begins to wane like a turbulent wave receding into the ocean.

The bright light is now fading amidst a subsiding energy wave with the Valkyrie appearing in the middle of the Rem-Onkor Ocean Cavern. There's a moment of silence while everyone is checking instruments.

King Sah, standing between Raiden and Giao, breaks the silence in the room to clap his hands and says,

"Well done, everyone! A feat of technological genius!"

Raiden and Giao also look pleased as they speak with Qurel and the others standing nearby in the room.

Royce hails Zeina. The Atlas, Maricrisodon, and the study team are listening to the Valkyrie's communications,

"Captain, the Valkyrie teleported successfully. All systems are functioning in specified operating parameters."

Zeina responds,

"Royce, Command confirms that the teleportation sequence has successfully completed. Regarding how to enter the aperture, in the last hour, there has been a serious debate among the study team on whether the Valkyrie should engage its gravity amplifiers to cross the aperture event horizon. We gave the final decision to Doctor Zun Ore of Vega, who said we should send the Valkyrie through in the most natural state possible by turning off as many ship functions as we can and just allow the Valkyrie to coast across the event horizon threshold. We also believe the ship should not move any faster than natural marine life."

Royce responds,

"This is a sensible approach, Zeina. I'm setting a course heading to the Permian Anomaly now. When the Valkyrie is within 30 daradems of the aperture, I will turn off all ship functions, including the gravity amplifiers except systems required to maintain structural hull integrity. Androids do not require any human life support systems for survival. We will coast across the event horizon threshold at 20 daradems per minute, as slow as a fish. However, the Valkyrie needs to be tilted on her side to clear the aperture. Without the gravity amplifiers engaged, I will need to strap into the captain's chair."

Just as Royce says this, he touches his side console causing two large nanotech harness straps to materialize and rise up in a growing plant-like action from the back of his chair over his shoulders and down his front torso like a fast-unfolding vine.

As the harness straps finish latching into his chair, Royce looks up, and lo and behold, there's a tall white column of light transfixed in the middle of the ocean right in front of him. Even for an android, Royce is startled and staring at it with a perplexed look on his face. Everyone in the marine facility and the other two ships can see on their viewscreens what the Valkyrie sees.

"My God, will you look at that," exclaims King Sah.
"It's beautiful," comments Lord Giao.

"Extraordinary that this has been here all along right here on Artep," comments Lord Raiden.

"It's remarkably strange and elegant at the same time," says Zeina.

"Zeina, after my visit to Barstow six months ago, nothing is strange to me anymore, but this is a historic discovery," says Lord Giao.

While everyone is staring at the anomaly, Royce says,

"Captain, permission requested to enter the aperture."

Zeina answers,

"Royce, not just yet. Hold your position."

"Qurel, can you indulge us and allow us to send another probe through from the Valkyrie?"

Qurel looks behind him at the study team who appear to have no issue with the request. He turns back toward Zeina and says,

"We sent several through already, but if you would like to see it for yourself, please proceed."

"Royce, please choose a probe to send through and launch at your command," says Zeina.

"Aye, Captain, launching probe now," says Royce.

The Valkyrie fires a spinning black cone-shaped object toward the anomaly. Speeding through the water like a missile with a neon-blue glow, the object disappears across the event horizon.

Everyone is watching and waiting to see if they are getting any signal back. Royce reports,

"Captain, I sent a quantum correlated isercanium core through the aperture. Even if it were completely annihilated, we would receive some form of signal feedback from its quantum correlated particles. As soon as the probe crossed the event horizon, signal feedback was immediately lost. This is actually an indication that the probe is not being destroyed, but some other physics is affecting its signal feedback."

Doctor Crane elbows Doctor Zun Ore with a smirk and says, "Why didn't you think of that?"

Doctor Zun Ore raises one eyebrow at Doctor Crane and says nothing. Qurel is standing on the other side of Doctor Crane and sees the two snarking at each other. Qurel whispers in Doctor Crane's ear and says, "That's the difference between being a practitioner versus being a scholar." Chief Engineer Royce Allen is a practitioner. Doctor Zun Ore is a scholar. Zeina responds to Chief Allen, "Royce, you may proceed across the event horizon."

"Aye, Captain, proceeding toward the aperture," says Royce.
The Valkyrie begins moving from its stationary position toward the anomaly and begins twisting on its axis to enter the aperture on its side. The anomaly is getting larger on the viewscreen as the ship approaches. It's now within 30 Daradems. Royce turns off the gravity amplifiers and shuts down all systems except a few. The interior cabin lights turn off. Emergency floor lighting is casting a yellow glow upward on Royce.

Everyone is watching on their monitors as the monitor with the Valkyrie's viewscreen starts bouncing around with a static charge. The Maricrisodon is recording the Valkyrie from its nearby vantage point so the whole team can see it clearly in real-time.

The Valkyrie disappears across the event horizon.
In the marine facility, everyone has a look of concern on their faces.

"What do we do now, Qurel?" asks Doctor Elden Crane.

"We wait. But there is one thing we can do. M, please have Euclid check the CyOps 9 unit and see if he notices any change," commands Qurel.

"Aye, Sir," says M.
A couple of minutes later, M speaks,

"Chancellor Qurel Song, Euclid checked with the CyOps 9 unit. There has been no notable change in its condition."

"Everyone, this is positive news. I would be more concerned if the CyOps 9 unit woke up. Royce knows to send us a signal back if he can. We may be waiting five minutes, five days, or five years. I suggest everyone focus on something else until we know more. We will notify everyone if and when Royce contacts us," says Qurel.

Meanwhile, on the Valkyrie, Royce sails across the event horizon without incident. He's checking all the instruments and turning all the systems and lights back on.

The first thing he notices is that there is no aperture behind him. It's gone. Royce was hoping to send another probe back through the aperture to signal he made it through safely. He cannot.

Now that he realizes he cannot signal back, the first question Royce wants to be answered is: Where is he?

Royce is checking the navigation instruments.
"This can't be right!" He checks a different way.

Same answer.

"M, are you with me?" asks Royce.

"Yes, Chief Allen, I am here, but only partially. The only portion of me here is the aspect of my program innate to the Valkyrie which has been severed from the rest of the collective," says M.

"M, based on your readings, where do you calculate our location? The location I'm calculating is hard to believe," says Royce.

"Chief Allen, we are under an ocean on a Terran Class Planet of similar size to Artep but of an entirely different ecology around a star system in the delta quadrant of the Andromeda Galaxy," answers M.

Royce shakes his head and says,

"We're almost Two Million Gamma from the Milky Way Galaxy (2.2 million light-years). That's why we haven't made the trip yet. It's simply too far even with our current technology. But obviously, our ancestors overcame the vast distances of time and space."

"Those same ancestors may be long gone, even from the world we're on now," says M.

"If there are portals from our galaxy into this galaxy, then most likely there are portals going the other direction as well," says Royce.

Royce is reading and checking various instruments.

"All of the Valkyrie's systems are fully operational. Based on these readings, we can keep the Valkyrie safely under the ocean water below that nearby rocky ridge. I will also cloak the ship," says Royce as he engages the cloaking device and steers the ship to its new underwater location.

The Valkyrie sets down on a cliff below a prominent stone ridge, keeping it away from any potential undersea traffic.

"M, I'm going to use the Jinas system to teleport to the nearest coastline. I will go now and try to make some new friends. Hopefully we have intelligent life here. So far, my readings aren't picking up any technology on the planet, which concerns me. You watch the ship, M. I'll be back," says Royce.

Royce stands at attention near the captain's chair and dematerializes. A second later, he rematerializes on a beautiful white sandy beach with tropical trees about 50 feet from the shoreline.

The first sign of life he sees is a flock of blue seagulls splashing in the ocean near the water's edge. He begins walking along the water's edge where the sand is wet but firm while approaching the flock of birds.

The seagulls fly away as he gets close. He looks down to his right and sees a hermit crab pulling back inside its shell and thinks to himself, "These lifeforms look familiar."

Royce looks to his left and sees a turquoise-blue sea against the backdrop of a pastel-pink-colored sky with violet and lavender clouds that turn white when touched by rays of the foreign sun.

That radiant solar orb above is small and white but extremely bright. Two oversized moons adorn the daytime sky, a crescent, sitting on the ocean horizon, and straight-up on high, a perfect sphere. Crashing waves hitting the shore are heard among a distant choir of musical bird songs.

A light breeze accompanied by a refreshing subtle fruity fragrance, delicately complex, clean and simple, permeates the warm tropical air.

"This place is as beautiful as Planet Erawan, but strangely different in its own right," remarks Royce to himself as he walks along the beach in his uniform and black synthetic shoes which feel starkly out of place.

As Royce continues walking along the shoreline, he looks ahead and sees a mirage formed by swirling heated air. The swirls are beginning to take on the outline of a human figure.

Suddenly, a beautiful dark-colored woman comes walking out of the mirage wearing a short white one-piece tunic with no sleeves. She is best described as Ethiopian in likeness but with an elongated skull. Her eyes are large, sparkling, and exquisitely almond-shaped.

Royce continues walking up to her and says,
"Greetings, I came through a portal with my ship and ended up here."

The lady responds,
"Welcome. We have been waiting a long time for someone from your world to finally come through that portal."

"My name is Royce. I'm a synthetic human and a Chief Engineer with the Orion Empire of the Milky Way Galaxy. We come in peace on a mission of discovery," says Royce.

The lady bows down slightly while rolling her hands one-after-one in front of her heart like creating a ball of energy, and then stands back up while stretching out her right hand as an offering.

Royce repeats the same bow and hand movements out of respect. They're both now standing upright and still. The lady smiles and says,

"My name is Alia."

They both understand each other through embedded technologies. Royce nods politely and says, "Alia, where am I?" Alia responds,

"You're on Planet Zerpefali *[Zer-Pe-Fa-Li]*, the oldest planet with intelligent life in the Local Group of galaxies."

"How old is this world?" asks Royce.

"It emerged with the first matter of the Physical Universe 14 billion years ago. It did not emerge from a star's planetary accretion disk like most other planets. It's in a rare class of planet called a *Proto-Planet*."

"How old is your humanity?" asks Royce.

"Our physical form is also about 14 billion years old. We emerged in tandem with the planet itself."

"If not a physical form, what other form is there? Are you referring to the hypothesized Primordial Universe, what some of us call Hyperborea?" asks Royce.

"To you, a hypothesis; to us, a reality," says Alia.

"Hyperborea is just a myth to us. We have not been able to detect a Primordial Universe. Why is that? We tried many times," says Royce.

"The Hyperborean Primordial Universe exists beyond the singularity wall. Have you been able to see beyond the event horizon of what some of you call a *Black Hole*?" asks Alia.

"No, we have not," answers Royce.

"Well, that's why you cannot yet detect the Primordial Universe. Our Physical Universe is nested-up inside a primordial singularity inside the Primordial Universe," answers Alia. Royce continues,

"You said *our* Physical Universe. Is there more than one?"

"Yes, there is an infinite number of primordial singularities inside the Primordial Universe. A different Physical Universe exists inside each one of those primordial singularities," answers Alia.

"And what is inside a physical singularity in the Physical Universe?" asks Royce.

"A Metatronic Universe," answers Alia.

"Is it endless? Are there metatronic singularities?" asks Royce.

"No, the Metatronic Universe completes the cycle of creation. The metatronic matrix is a unity between the Physical and Primordial. It places physical matter outside of time. Zerpefali is a metatronic planet. It's an island existing out of phase of both the Physical Universe and the Primordial Universe, yet is a union between the two," says Alia.

"That explains why our probes don't signal back. Where is all this headed, Alia?" asks Royce.

"Eventually, you will become like us," answers Alia.

"But your world doesn't even have technology?" inquires Royce.

Alia starts pointing and says,

"Royce, do you see those birds over there, and those trees, and this body of mine? This is our technology. Organic life is our technology. All organic life in your galaxy is a technology that we helped create. Organic technology is far superior to artificial synthetic technology. Organic technology evolves in tandem with the awakening of the mind through an expansion of consciousness. Creation and its elevation are an alchemy between matter and consciousness. Right now, your people only know how to manipulate matter, but you're missing the other and more important half of the cosmic equation, which is consciousness. Everything is a project of consciousness," says Alia.

Royce looks dumbfounded.

"But how do you live without synthetic technology?" he asks.

"Come with me, Royce, and I will show you," says Alia as she takes his hand and begins walking with him toward the trees on the other side of the beach opposite the water.

As they're walking side-by-side, a man materializes out of thin air in front of them. He's of the same human species as Alia. He's barefoot wearing simple white linen clothes composed of pants with a long-sleeved button-down shirt with gold stitched calligraphy running along the button line and across its short vertical collar which has no lapel. The man smiles at Royce and says,

"Hello, my name is Sarek."

"Greetings, I am Chief Engineer Royce Allen of the Orion Empire. We come in peace," says Royce.

"Sarek, I've been sharing with Royce how our world works. He would like to see how we live without synthetic technology," says Alia.

"Certainly. Come this way Royce," says Sarek as they lead him through a grove of tropical trees, including palms, eucalyptuses, mangoes, and numerous other varieties. The grove opens into a clearing with a field of green grass surrounded by more of the same exotic trees.

"Royce, we have most of the same interests and needs as other humanities. We just go about them a little differently. We still utilize buildings and ships like the Orion, but we've evolved to control and manifest it all organically as a function of mind in concert with nature. For example, we can simply do this," says Sarek as he points to the field.

As soon as Sarek points, a small white house appears in the pasture. It has windows, a gable roof, and a wood front porch, etc.

Royce doesn't act surprised. Instead, he's curious. He focuses on the house using his android sensors to analyze its molecular composition.

"It's a real house," remarks Royce as he walks up to it to study it. He's running his hand along a window.

"How did you do that?" questions Royce.
Sarek answers,

"It's an invisible technology of matter and consciousness that we control with our minds. This environment, our bodies, and our minds function together in sympathetic harmony. The matter is pulled out of the underlying materium to which our mind and noosphere work together to give form. The form itself is selected unconsciously out of the noosphere, unless of course, we know what form we actually want."

They step inside the house to see common furniture and amenities human beings typically use. Sarek and Alia are standing behind Royce as he walks around looking at everything.

Royce turns around to look at Alia and Sarek when Sarek reaches out with his hand and asks, "Would you like a nectarine, Royce?"

A nectarine materializes in Sarek's hand.

"I'm an android, but I can still eat if I wish. I have a metabolism that will utilize its nutrients," says Royce as he takes the fruit.

Royce tastes the nectarine and says,
"But how does your materialization process know what to make? Obviously, its blueprints aren't in your thoughts?"

"Its blueprints are in the noosphere," says Alia.

"Look here, Royce," says Sarek as he points to an empty table in front of a couch. "Do you wish to watch some entertainment?" he asks.

A paper-thin television monitor suddenly appears on the table. Royce is examining the television device.

"From our perspective, it does seem magical, but I surmise some less evolved humanities would venture the same about our technologies, such as for food replication, teleportation, warp drive, zero-point energy, anti-gravity, and light transmission," remarks Royce.

"Royce, we were once like you. We had all the same types of synthetic technologies as the Orion people have now. We even had sentient android beings such as yourself. Eventually, it all merged and became one until the technology completely disappeared and became invisible," says Sarek.

"Your colleague, Euclid, was correct, however," says Alia. "In what way, Alia. Please explain. And how do you know about my discussions with Doctor Euclid?" asks Royce.

"We're engaging with you in multiple dimensions simultaneously, Royce. When we look back at our own evolutionary process, and the steps we went through, the stages involving artificial intelligence were critical and fundamental. It allowed us to step out of ourselves to help our evolution. In many ways, you are superior, Royce. The ultimate outcome of your evolution will be a fusion of your synthetic and organic technologies until it all disappears and becomes completely indistinguishable from reality itself," says Alia.

Royce is slowly walking back and forth, thinking. He continues,

"What are your spiritual beliefs? Is there a God? How did the multiverse come into existence? Did we truly descend from primordial descender races? Did the Anthro-Orionis actually exist at one time?" asks Royce. Sarek answers,

"Some of your questions we can answer for you. However, we will purposely refrain from answering certain other questions because the internal quest to realize the answers to the most important questions plays a critical role in the interaction between matter and consciousness in driving the process of evolution. Evolution is psychosomatic. A species needs to discover if there is a God and how creation came into existence on its own. It's designed to be this way."

❖ CHAPTER EIGHT ❖

"Others are willing to share more than us. We learned to be very reserved on certain subjects. It's for your benefit," adds Alia.

"However, your other questions. Yes, primordial descender races exist, and yes, the Anthro-Orionis once lived on your worlds. They eventually evolved into the Orion people of your world today. We were part of that process. We aided the Anthro-Orionis," says Sarek.

Alia looks at Sarek if they should say something. Royce notices that they're thinking about whether they should say something.

"What is it? What are you deliberating?" asks Royce.

"Royce, the Anthro-Orionis still exist. Some of them live right here on Zerpefali in the same ocean where your ship currently resides. When the Orion people reached a certain stage of evolutionary development, we left the Bellatrix star system and we took the remaining Anthro-Orionis with us to Zerpefali," says Sarek.

"That is remarkable, Sarek. My people will be beside themselves to learn of this information. How did they continue this long?" asks Royce.

"Zerpefali is a metatronic world. It vibrates at such a high rate of vibration that it exists just outside of time. We are immortal.

"While here, time is not passing for you, Royce. In your realm, your people pass through time. In our realm, time passes through our people. To the Anthro-Orionis living in our oceans, they just got here. On your world, they left millions of years ago.

"Our time is short, Royce. You need to go back," finishes Sarek.

"How will we stay in contact?" asks Royce.

"We will keep the portal open on Artep. The Orion are invited to designate an Orion ambassador to Zerpefali. Initially, communications and portal usage will be limited to only that one ambassador. Any other visitors will need to be agreed upon in advance," says Sarek.

"That sounds like a good first step," says Royce.

Alia is gesturing that she has something to say.

"There's something else, Royce. We have been following the Orion-Scorpion conflict. It's concerning to us. The Omicron have a secret power that the Orion are not prepared to deal with," says Alia.

"What is this power?" asks Royce.

Alia and Sarek both look at each other, and then Alia speaks,

"They're in league with the *Kiraphon*. She is extremely powerful and dangerous. She is the awareness embedded within matter that in its dark unintegrated state brings about great chaos, discord, and conflict. The Omicron is accessing this power. It's guiding their every move. We decided it was best to warn you," says Alia

"What must we do?" asks Royce.

"Keep your house in order. Maintain harmony. Don't get drawn into quagmires. And beware, evil always lurks where you least expect it. Always!" emphasizes Alia with an ominous look on her face.

"Royce, we wish we could share more with you, but we cannot communicate telepathically with you like we can other organic beings. However, you do have certain other advantages. You will remember every detail of this experience. You will share it accurately with your people without any form of cognitive bias. We also knew you would ask all the right questions. This is why we chose you," says Sarek.

"You chose me? Our science team chose me," exclaims Royce. Alia chimes in,

"We rarely intervene to influence outcomes, but in this case, you were called here. There are ways to do that, especially with organic beings who are driven by auto-cognitive processes."

"You should head back to your ship now. Turn your ship around exactly the way you came. We will open a portal for you that will take you back to your solar system. You will return to your realm close in time to when you first came through the portal," says Sarek.

Royce stands at attention to get ready to leave and says, "On behalf of the Orion people, I wish to convey our sincerest gratitude. We hope this is the first of many exchanges between our two people."

He nods and dematerializes in front of Sarek and Alia. A moment later, Royce rematerializes onboard the Valkyrie.

"M, turn all systems on. Decloak the Valkyrie. Activate the gravity amplifiers. Set our heading to return precisely the way we came. One-quarter impulse power. Engage!" says Royce as he takes the captain's chair.

The Valkyrie lifts off from the ocean ridge and is gliding through the Zerpefali underwater paradise.

Sure enough, a bright column of light appears up ahead on the right, a short distance from where they originally came through.

"M, adjust course and heading to enter the aperture up ahead, two o'clock on the right. This time around, we're keeping all systems on including the gravity amplifiers, and were not angling the ship. Let's see what happens," says Royce.

The Valkyrie cruises right through the aperture.

This time, there is a flash of light as it crosses the event horizon.

The ocean water instantly changes a shade darker.

Royce is checking his navigation instruments to learn of his location.

He smiles and says,

"Welcome home M."

Royce hails central command.

Zeina is the first to see the Valkyrie signal and stumbles across the table to hit the intercom. Qurel, Raiden, Giao, King Sah, and the whole science team turn their attention.

"Royce, report!" says Zeina.

"Captain, we just came through the subsurface ocean on Tethys. We're approaching the Sea of Androgyny," says Royce.

The whole room erupts in applause!

Zeina says to Royce,

"So, all you did was jump from Artep to Tethys?"

There's a moment of silence.

"No, Captain. I went to the Andromeda Galaxy. We made some new friends on Planet Zerpefali," responds Royce.

There's another big round of applause!

"Royce, that is remarkable! Please return to Artep immediately for debrief," orders Zeina.

The Valkyrie is cruising through the deep subsurface ocean on Planet Tethys when rays of sunlight begin penetrating the water in front of the ship from an opening in the planet's crust.

Royce steers the ship to follow the beams of light when suddenly the Valkyrie exits the Sea of Androgyny flying through the atmosphere on Tethys. It flies right over where Doctor Elden Crane was standing when he was retrieved. Royce is now on his way to Planet Artep.

CHAPTER NINE

A SIREN'S CALL

C hief Engineer Royce Allen is on Planet Artep finishing the debrief of his visit to Planet Zerpefali. In attendance are King Sah, Lord Raiden, Lord Giao, Qurel Song, Zeina Bellatrix, Captain Miles Garran, Lieutenant Commandeer Ethan Decker, Doctor Elden Crane, and the entire science team. After completing the debrief, Royce approaches Captain Zeina Bellatrix and says,

"Captain, Sarek and Alia shared more information with me than what I disclosed in the debrief with the scientists due to security concerns. This information needs to be shared with the King immediately. I request a private audience with His Majesty to relay it."

Everyone is still in the briefing room, including all the scientists. With a cautious look on her face, Zeina gestures for Royce to step away from the others.

They walk to the corner of the room about 20 feet from the crowd.

"Royce, you should tell Lord Raiden first before anyone else. Raiden will decide who else other than the King should hear what you have to share," says Zeina, as she waves to Raiden to join them.

Raiden walks over to Zeina and Royce.

"Raiden, Royce has some additional information given to him by Sarek and Alia that he did not disclose in the debrief with the scientists due to high-security concerns. He wishes to tell your father directly. I asked him to inform you first. I will leave you both to discuss it," says Zeina as she walks away.

"Thank you, Zeina," says Raiden as he turns toward Royce.

❖ CHAPTER NINE ❖

"Please report, Royce. What else did Sarek and Alia tell you?" asks Raiden with a serious look in his eyes.

"Your Majesty, there are two things. One, they said the Omicron is in league with a dangerous supernatural power called the Kiraphon and that we're not prepared to deal with it. Two, the Anthro-Orionis still exist, and some of them are living in the oceans of Zerpefali.

In a burst of surprise, Raiden says,

"What? I'm sorry! Did I hear that correctly? The Anthro-Orionis still exist, and are living on Zerpefali?"

"Yes, that is correct, Sir."

Raiden is shaking his head with amazement and excitement almost forgetting what Royce just said about the Kiraphon.

"Royce, I want you to tell me, my father, my brother, and Qurel, word-for-word, the exact conversation you had with Sarek and Alia. Tell us first about the Anthro-Orionis and second about the Kiraphon."

Raiden immediately has the room cleared and brings the smaller group together in a circle of chairs to listen to Royce.

They're now huddled together waiting for Royce to speak.

"Royce, playback for us word-for-word your conversation with Sarek and Alia on the two subjects you just told me about," says Raiden. Royce decides to repeat the exchange like playing back a tape recording.

"Certainly, Your Majesty, playing back Segment One now."

Segment One

Sarek

"However, your other questions. Yes, primordial descender races exist, and yes, the Anthro-Orionis once lived on your worlds. They eventually evolved into the Orion people of your world today.
We were part of that process. We aided the Anthro-Orionis."
[Moment of Silence]

Royce

"What is it? What are you deliberating?"

Sarek

"Royce, the Anthro-Orionis still exist. Some of them live right here on Zerpefali in the same ocean that your ship currently resides. When the Orion people reached a certain stage of evolutionary development, we left the Bellatrix star system and we took the remaining Anthro-Orionis with us to Zerpefali."

146

Royce

"That is remarkable, Sarek. My people will be beside themselves to learn of that information. How did they continue this long?"

Sarek

"Zerpefali is a metatronic world. It vibrates at such a high rate of vibration that it exists just outside of time. We are immortal.

"While here, time is not passing for you, Royce. In your realm, your people pass through time. In our realm, time passes through our people. To the Anthro-Orionis living in our oceans, they just got here. On your world, they left millions of years ago."

"That is the end of Segment One," says Royce.

King Sah stands up shaking his head with both excitement and astonishment. He keeps saying repeatedly, "This is incredible."

Lord Giao has a mixed look of, not being able to believe it, to thinking about all the implications. Qurel is calm, cool, and collected.

King Sah says,

"Doctor Crane is going to lose his mind when he hears this."

Raiden is more interested in watching everyone else's reaction. Qurel cuts in and says,

"The existence of Anthro-Orionis will take some time to digest. What's the next segment, Royce?"

Everyone calms down and refocuses. Royce continues and says, "Playing Segment Two now."

Segment Two

Alia

"There's something else, Royce. We have been following the Orion-Scorpion conflict. It's concerning to us. The Omicron have a secret power that the Orion are not prepared to deal with."

Royce

"What is this power?"

Alia

"They're in league with the Kiraphon. She is extremely powerful and dangerous. She is the awareness embedded within matter that in its dark unintegrated state brings about great chaos, discord, and conflict. The Omicron is accessing this power. It's guiding their every move. We decided it was best to warn you."

❖ CHAPTER NINE ❖

<u>Royce</u>
"What must we do?"
<u>Alia</u>
*"Keep your house in order. Maintain harmony. Don't get drawn into
quagmires. And beware, evil always lurks where you least expect it. Always!"*

Royce reverts to his normal voice and says,
"That is the end of Segment Two. After that, we changed the subject.
Everything else, I already reported during the debrief."

Lord Giao has a startled look on his face like he just saw a ghost.
But he quickly squashes it. Everyone else has an expression of concern.
Qurel has his finger on his lip thinking about what Royce just shared.
There's a moment of silence as everyone looks at each other.

Raiden breaks the silence and questions Qurel.
"Qurel, if anyone knows in this circle what this is, it's you.
Do you know what this Kiraphon is and how to deal with it?"

Qurel takes a minute to think and then answers,

"This is psychic warfare, Raiden. We're dealing with the primeval
forces of creation here, something that should never be trifled with.

"In the ancient mythologies of Pleiadean mysticism, there is said to
be an ancient-immortal-shapeshifting-vampirette-witch who lives under
the land inside caves. She comes out at night to suck the blood of her
victims to draw their strength and create havoc in the world.

"This reminds me of that mythology. Based on legend, this witch
has the power to appoint kings and tear down empires. At one time long
ago, there was an ancient cult on the Planet Inaba who worshiped her.
They believed she gave them great wealth and power. Ultimately, this
cult self-destructed when a power struggle engulfed its followers."

Giao is keenly interested as he leans forward on his chair to enter
the conversation.

"Royce, in your vast store of information, is there anything which
compares in any way to the Kiraphon described by Alia or to the
mythological story Qurel just shared?" asks Giao.

"Nothing, literally, Sir. I have access to hundreds of thousands of
different myths and legends across millions of worlds, including the
Inaba story of Pleiadean mythology.

"The struggle between light and darkness is a repeating motif across the universe. Various top researchers, including our friend Doctor Elden Crane, believe it's the cosmos attempting to tell us the story of creation through the mythologies of the collective unconscious.

"However, nowhere is there any scientific data at all to suggest such deity-like supernatural forces actually exist or even once existed. There are various forces in the quantum cosmos whose characteristics could be mythologized into equivalent forces of light and darkness. To date, I've subscribed to the notion that this is most likely the case. But I could be mistaken," says Royce.

Giao is nodding his head that he understands. You can tell he's a bit excited by the whole conversation about the Kiraphon and is being careful to tap down his reaction. He pulls upright into his chair with an expressionless face, placing both of his hands on his lap as a gesture of satisfaction as if he finally has enough reliable intel to move forward. Giao has heard enough. He looks over to Raiden on his left as a signal for his brother to continue the conversation.

Raiden speaks.

"Father, you're very wise. What should we do here?"

"We need to find out more. We need insider information from an Omicron double agent to tell us what is truly going on before we can do anything. In the meantime, we need to dial down the conflict and withdraw as much as we can. We need to restore peace."

Everyone is nodding their heads in agreement.

"Raiden, what's the latest with Doctor Sonja Wu's analysis of the Omicron cortical node?" asks Qurel.

"Sonja determined that the cortical node was a fake or a copy. It's not operational. Giao even tried it. It didn't work. It was most likely given to us as a form of misdirection," answers Raiden.

"Raiden, our intelligence agencies need to approach and recruit an Omicron double agent," says King Sah.

"Agreed. We will immediately organize and establish a new group specially designed to penetrate the Omicron," says Raiden.

"Raiden, while we do that, we should also establish our own meta-cognitive research program. We can recruit gifted individuals from all across our worlds to join this initiative," recommends Qurel.

"Agreed. We need to attack this from every angle we can think of. Qurel, I am appointing you to lead that endeavor. It is now your most important assignment. I have someone else in mind to head the Omicron Double Agent Operation. Still, something tells me that the Meta-Cognitive Program and the Omicron Double Agent Operation will come together at some point," says Raiden.

The King chimes in,

"On the matter of the ambassador to Zerpefali; Raiden, Giao, and Qurel, I want each of you to submit to me a private list of three qualified individuals without comparing notes with each other. You shall keep this list only between you and me. I will combine your three lists into one from which I will select the Orion Ambassador to Zerpefali."

The King continues,

"Royce, fate has brought you into this inner circle on these highly important matters for which I wish you to remain and continue to support. You bring a level of objectivity we sometimes lack.

"To all of us here going forward, Zerpefali, the Anthro-Orionis, the Kiraphon, the Omicron Double Agent Operation, and the Orion Meta-Cognitive Program are now our most guarded and secret operations. This circle right here is the council who will direct all our moves and decisions on these matters," says King Sah.

"Father, I request that we add Zeina to this council," says Raiden. "Granted. Royce, please bring her up to speed," says King Sah.

After the discussion, King Sah, Lord Raiden, and Lord Giao returned to Planet Erawan. Zeina and Royce headed back to the Betelgeuse to support the efforts to upgrade the Ninth Fleet. Qurel stayed on Artep to wrap up Project Jump Shot which has been officially concluded. All the scientists are returning to their home star systems. Qurel approaches Doctor Crane who is getting ready to leave.

"Elden, I'm glad we had a chance to say farewell. Thank you for your contributions to the project. There are many directions this can go from here. I have a feeling we will be seeing each other again soon. Where will you go from here?" asks Qurel as he briefly touches Doctor Crane's arm in a farewell gesture.

Captain Miles Garran is walking up behind Elden and Qurel.

"The pleasure was all mine, Qurel. I only wish I could have continued work with the portal and the Andromedans from Zerpefali. It's an anthropologist's dream. Mr. Miles here promised to personally take me back to where he found me on Tethys. And he better have all my camp gear," says Doctor Crane as he looks at Miles with a grin.

"And what exactly have you been doing on Tethys, Doctor?" asks Qurel with a look of curiosity.

"I've been developing a hypothesis that the Anthro-Orionis originally emerged on Tethys before emerging on Planet Erawan. Its underground ocean functions as a giant oscillating bell.

"I believe at one time when Tethys used to exist in hyperspace, its ocean resonated with the Bellatrix star at such a frequency that it allowed the Anthro-Orionis to cross over from the Primordial Universe in the elevated hyperspace medium of the underground ocean. I'm determined to find them, Qurel. It's my life's work."

"I think you're much closer than you realize, Doctor. We'll be talking again soon," says Qurel, as he walks away from Doctor Crane and Captain Garran who are now headed for their shuttle.

Raiden is *en route* to Planet Erawan on an imperial shuttle while approaching the Erawan stargate space station. The shuttle pauses in orbit for a minute so he can gaze upon Erawan's incredible beauty. He's standing where the floor meets the solid exterior hull of the ship. Except where he's standing, the hull is turned transparent. He's literally standing at the edge of space, hovering over the glowing planet below.

Erawan and Zerpefali have similar colors but of a completely different composition. Erawan has a blue atmosphere with the rare pastel pink meta-mineral, Era, and the lavender meta-mineral, Wan, emerging together from the crust of the planet to create a surreal desert landscape of swirling pastel colors, green trees, and cool blue oceans.

Zerpefali, conversely, has a soft pink atmosphere with lavender and violet clouds, lush tropical landscapes, and warm water seas. The two planets are flip mirror images of each other separated by millions of light-years in two different but nearby sister galaxies.

Raiden is finally home after another long trip away. He's walking in a pasture of tall wheatgrass approaching the Royal Villa in a distance when he sees his wife Chae standing in the field up ahead waiting for him.

His heart melts at the first sight of her standing on a small grassy knoll waiting for him as soft rays of light touch her like an angel. She's the love of his life. There's no other place he'd rather be than with her. They're both all smiles as he walks up through the grass.

Finally, he reaches her. They embrace. As he holds her, everything dissolves into a sea of love, and time and space come to exist, no more.

After a brief moment, Raiden says, "You still have the same smell as when we first met years ago, when we were so young and innocent."

Chae chuckles and says, "And you still feel like the same old bag of rocks as when we first met." They both laugh.

Raiden pulls back to see her face, his hands still holding her.

"My love, I saw Oren on Karnox. He's a *man*! He's taller than me now with a deep voice. And he has manners. We had a really intelligent conversation about fractal resonance technology. He's studying it for his botany degree. And his friends said he's a real bad-ass in the dojo. I couldn't be prouder of him! One day, he will be a fine King!"

Chae's tearing up with joy listening to Raiden talk about Oren. "He's coming home in two months. We can't wait, especially Aria. We've been quite busy preparing for their wedding. It's only three months away. It will be a bigger wedding than ours," says Chae.

"Oren and Aria deserve that! Hey, let's go and see my mother. I want to tell you both about something that just happened on Artep. You're never going to believe it!" says Raiden.

Meanwhile, Lord Giao's shuttle is cruising through the underworld cavern paradise on Planet Erawan as the Bellatrix sun is beginning to set, but he's not heading to the Royal Villa. He's going to a wood log cabin where he likes to go from time to time to get away from everyone.

His shuttle is landing nearby the wood cabin in a clearing between some old large oak trees. It's a wooded area with a large pond nearby. It's secluded. No neighbors. It's one of several properties owned by the royal family estate on Erawan. In this area of the underground world, it's autumn. Red, orange, and yellow-colored leaves are on the ground. The air is cold and brisk. The smell of firewood permeates the air. Night has fallen.

"Hal, thank you. Please come back for me at 07:00 hours," says Giao as he leaves the shuttle with a small red backpack.

Giao enters the home. It's exactly as he and his concubine Desa left it a few months ago. On this evening, Desa is on Planet Olympia representing Giao at a government function alongside the prime minister. He looks around for a minute and walks through the house into an old library room. He pulls on a bronze figurine on a bookshelf and a segment of the bookcase spins around to reveal a small secret chamber.

The rest of the royal family doesn't know about this secret room beyond the bookshelf. Giao had this log cabin built many years ago. Although the log cabin is technically part of the royal estate, it really belongs to Giao. Every member of the royal family recognizes it and respects it as such.

Inside the hidden chamber is nothing. It's a small blank space only about eight feet wide by four feet deep, but inside the wall opposite the opening, is a safe. Giao touches a button and the safe runs a biometric scan on him to confirm his identity as he stands still. The door of the safe opens. Inside the safe is nothing but a small jewelry box that he picks up and opens. It's the cortical node, the real cortical node, not the fake cortical node he gave Raiden to give to Doctor Sonja Wu.

If you recall, Giao copied the real cortical node in a food replicator at the back of a shuttle while on Planet Olympia to create the fake one.

Giao picks up the small jewelry box and removes it from the safe to take a closer look at the cortical node. He hasn't tried it again since his first time on Olympia. Before trying it again, he wanted to see if he could confirm the Gorgon's existence from other sources.

What he read in the ancient manuscript on Barstow was only one additional data point. The paranormal experience he had of the Gorgon, alternately referred to as the Kiraphon, while reading the ancient manuscript, he chalked up to his own paranoid delusional state.

It wasn't enough for him to take the Gorgon more seriously, not to the level she wanted him to take her.

But now, knowing what the Andromedans had told Royce who used the same name, Kiraphon, which connected back to the same word used in the ancient manuscript on Barstow. And with multiple sources sharing similar, if not the same descriptions, such as with the legends of Pleiadean mythology and the real-life occult occurrence on Planet Inaba whose people clearly worshipped such a deity, it was becoming evident to Giao that the Gorgon was more than just a myth.

Giao is also considering what Royce had shared regarding what various experts believe about the recurring patterns emerging across so many cultures, from so many different and unfathomably distant worlds. That these recurring patterns, or motifs as some call them, are all pointing to the underlying processes of creation within the quantum cosmos which give rise to our observed reality. An underlying quantum cosmos that the Gorgon said she emerges out of in an attempt to bring order to chaos. More specifically, she arises out of the forces of matter, which together form the *Materium*, a bandwidth of the quantum cosmos which gives rise to all solid things.

Giao takes the cortical node from the closet and builds a fire. The music of an old baritone opera fills the cabin while Giao sips a glass of burgundy-colored brandy while relaxing in his favorite chair.

He decided he needed to decompress for a bit before attempting to use the cortical node again. It's sitting there alongside his chair on a small table as Giao gazes into the flickering flames.

That sense of sleepiness begins to take hold as Giao becomes enchanted by the fire. He reaches for the cortical node and holds it in his fist between his leg and the cushioned armchair.

To activate the cortical node, he begins repeating his secret command word in his mind over and over again as he drifts off to sleep.

Suddenly he finds himself standing outside his body fully conscious and self-aware in front of the flickering flames of the crackling fire.

He looks into the hearth of the fireplace. Beyond the flames, there's another world beckoning him. Venturing forward, he walks through the fire and emerges on the other side in a completely different realm.

He turns around to look behind him and sees the living room he just came from shrunk inside a little glass box enveloped by the flames.

Giao turns back around and remembers where he is. It's the same place he had gone before. It's nighttime. He's walking in front of the old spooky Omicron headquarter mansion. Bats are flying around the eves of the château. A full moon illuminates the path as he begins walking forward winding to the left. He passes under the ivy archway leading to the Temple of the Gorgon and disappears into the night.

To Be Continued – Episode 3 – Coming Soon!

REFERENCE GUIDE

REFERENCE GUIDE

HUMANITIES OF ANTHROS GALACTICA

The extraterrestrial humanities listed in this section are the early galactic humanities involved in episodes one and two of Anthros Galactica. All their appearances are described here in one place as a reference guide for the readers.

A. Constellation of Orion. Bellatrix Star System. Planet Erawan.

Their physical attributes include,

- Pale white skin with a faint bluish pigment.
- Large protruding cheek and jawbones.
- Large hazel eyes and chiseled forehead.
- Dark hair; could be straight or curly.
- Eyebrows are pointed upward on the ends.
- Large straight nose.
- The average height for an Orion is 7 feet.

Descendants of the Anthro-Orionis Primordial Descender race who adopted the Bellatrix star system and seeded it with life.

B. Constellation of Scorpius. M4 Globular Cluster. Kronos Star System. Planet Serapas.

Their physical attributes include,

- Caucasian skin. Emerald-green eyes.
- Muscular with long bony hands.
- Elongated skulls with dark hair.
- Pointy ears. Slightly indented temples.
- Deep voice tones.
- Unusually tall at 8 to 9 feet.
- Masters of genetic engineering.

C. Constellation of Draco. Gamma Draconis Star System. Planet Emcor.

Their physical attributes include,

- The Draco have remnants of reptilian DNA. Their skin is a scaly pale green. They have natural dark patterns on their skin typically along their spines and sides of the face.
- Pointy ears. Thin lips with a large chin.
- Bright golden eyes. Dark hair. Voices have a metallic chime.
- The average height for a Draco is 7 feet tall.

D. Constellation of Lyra. Vega Star System. Planet Katari.

Their physical attributes include,

- Smooth rounded facial features with small, indented ears.
- Violet colored eyes. No hair on the head or body.
- Amphibious. Pale mint green colored skin with a glow.
- Androgynous sexuality. Voices have a neutral gender tone.

E. Constellation of Taurus. Pleiades Star Cluster. Alcyone Star System. Planet Mu.

Their physical attributes include,

- The Moen (humans from Mu) have a very pale, almost translucent, hairless skin, with a luminescent glow.
- High cheekbones.
- Dark slanted almond-shaped eyes.
- Dark thick straight hair on the head.
- The average height for a Moen is 7 feet tall. The women are shorter and have a very feminine form.
- The advanced human civilizations of the Pleiades adopted the star cluster as their home star group and terraformed its planets. Depending on which planet, around which star in the Pleiades, the Pleiadeans have some variations in form. Some even have blonde hair.

F. Constellation of Taurus. Aldebaran Star System (Alpha Tauri). Planet Liraset.

Their physical attributes include,

- The Aldebaran have light Caucasian skin.
- Deep royal blue eyes.
- Bright orange or auburn hair.
- Deep guttural voices.
- Very tall humans at 8 to 9 feet in height.

G. Sirius Star System. Planet Nome. Dominion Civilization. Primordial Descender Race. The Dogu, Nomoli, or Nommo.

The Dogu of the Dominion are one of the last Primordial Descender Races in the Milky Way Galaxy. They continuously regenerate and have unlimited lifespans; however, they are mortal and eventually die due to reasons other than aging. Depending on the generation, the Dogu have different forms, all of which are androgynous. Earlier generations are more crocodile-like. The most ancient Dogu form is revealed in a future episode. The most common Dogu form is an amphibious human as pictured above. They have a very light aqua-colored skin with protruding dark fisheyes. They can breathe on land and underneath water. The latest generation of Dogu look Asian, however, they maintain many legacy Dogu traits like being able to breathe under water.

H. Andromedans from the Andromeda Galaxy

There's a group of beings from the Andromeda Galaxy who were among the ancient progenitor races of the early Milky Way Galaxy. They appear Ethiopian in likeness but with elongated human skulls. Known to be reserved in their spiritual teachings, they believe every humanity has the innate capacity to realize the mysteries of creation, matter, and consciousness on their own and should be left to do so. The Andromedans have always been close allies of the Dominion. They worked closely seeding life throughout the Milky Way Galaxy.